# ROADKILL JUSTICE

### Featuring

*Yooper Woodswoman*
*Nettie Bramble*

# Terri Martin

Modern History Press

Ann Arbor, MI

Roadkill Justice: Featuring Yooper Woodswoman Nettie Bramble

ISBN 978-1-61599-774-9 paperback
ISBN 978-1-61599-775-6 hardcover
ISBN 978-1-61599-776-3 eBook

Published by
Modern History Press          www.ModernHistoryPress.com
5145 Pontiac Trail            info@ModernHistoryPRess.com
Ann Arbor, MI 48105

Tollfree 888-761-6268 (USA/CAN)
FAX 734-663-6861

Distributed by Ingram Book Group (USA/CAN/AU/UK)

Dedicated to those Woodswomen (and men)

who live slightly off the grid.

Also by the Author

*Children's*

The Home Wind (age 9+)

Voodoo Shack: A Michigan Mystery (age 8+)

*Adult*

*Short Stories-Humor*

Church Lady Chronicles: Devilish Encounters

High on the Vine: Featuring Yooper Entrepreneurs Tami & Evi Maki

*Full Length Novel*

Moose Willow Mystery

# Contents

## Hook, Line & Stinker

Me and Ma live off the land. That and her government check. My name's Nettle Bramble, but folks call me Nettie for short and it just burns my kindling that a body's gotta have a license to put food on the table. I call it substance living. My snooty sister, MarshMarigold, says it's more like sub-standard living. Just because her husband, Tag Alder, has his own septic pumping business—he calls it Tag's Honey Wagon—and makes a bundle out of sucking up folks' you-know-what, doesn't mean that using what God puts there for the taking isn't a fair way to live. I'd much rather be in the woods or on a lake somewhere than to be driving that smelly ol' truck around and charging folks to tear up their lawn and stink up the neighborhood.

Me and Ma have an outhouse and when the pit gets full, we fill in the hole and dig us a new one then move the outhouse over it. Not my favorite thing to do, mind you, but it smells a whole lot better'n that truck of Tag's. He's had a lot of complaints from the neighbors about parking the Honey Wagon in his driveway, so he's been putting the thing in the gravel pit a ways from me and Ma's cabin. Tag pays Ma with a few bottles of hooch for the deal.

What croaks my goat is that I gotta get a license to catch a fish or take down a critter for supper. Might as well go to a fancy restaurant and have someone else do the catching and cleaning for what a license costs. Well, maybe I mean what a license would cost if I bothered to get one, which I don't. Not that I don't strictly abide by the rules of the woods and water. I only take what is plentiful and eat what I take. Mostly.

Can't say the same for my sister's two brats, Wanton and Wiley, who get a plate of food then commence to waste half of it. The Alder clan showed up just as I was getting ready to go fishin' wanting me and Ma to sit the two boys for a weekend while she and Tag went off on some lovey dovey trip where I figure they don't want their whiny kids around. Ma tolerates her grandsons because they're family plus the older one favors my pa—rest in peace—and that makes Ma a little soft on him. What it boils down to is that Ma squirms out of it and leaves the babysitting to me. But I go along with it because I've been trying to turn my wimpy nephews into *real boys*.

"Eeewww!" Wiley, the younger one squealed at the idea of digging up worms. Now most boys (and some girls, too) just love crawling around in the dirt looking for worms, which is what you gotta do before you go pole fishing at the creek. When I use my rod and reel, I prefer Circus Peanuts and pork fat for bait, but for catching a couple of catfish, which are your bottom feeders, you need a fishpole and worms. No way am I paying for worms any more than I'm paying for a fishin' license, so I sent the boys out behind the shed to dig up some crawlers. Ma promised to fry up the fish for us if we had any luck. You'd a thunk I sent my girly nephews out to bury a body or something the way they dragged butt. So I went to show 'em how it's done and maybe play a little trick too.

"See, boys, you just put the shovel metal part pointing at the ground and push with your foot," I said. Lord, they didn't even know what the business end of a shovel was. The older one managed to dig up a few inches of dirt before saying he was tuckered out.

"Ya know, Wanton—and you too, Wiley—I didn't want to tell yous before, but I'll let you in on a secret. I heard that folks are getting a lot of gold nuggets out of the creek by huntin' for them with a fishpole and worms. Story is that my grandpa caught enough gold outa the creek to buy up this land me and Ma live on!"

"Yeah?" said the younger one.

"Uh huh," I said. "Your granny and me have been waiting for some smart fellas like you boys to help us get more nuggets outa the creek and we can split up the money they bring. You wouldn't need to go to school anymore 'cause you'd be rich."

"But I like school," said the older one.

"Me too," said the younger one.

"That so? Well you'd be smart and rich then!"

"Yeah!" Wanton said digging with more enthusiasm. "I'll buy an ATV."

"Me too," Wiley said, dropping to his knees to inspect the clumps of dirt. "There's some worms in here, Aunt Nettie!"

"Well, get them out and put them in the cans and we'll head to the creek to catch us some gold nuggets."

Lickety-split we had us a couple of coffee cans full of fat nightcrawlers and was headed down the two-track road to the creek. Normally when I go to the creek, I try to move along quiet so's not to draw attention to myself, being without a license and all. But the boys were excited about finding gold and they made a lot of racket and that attracted unwanted attention from the local conservation officer, Will Ketchum. CO Ketchum is what you would call over-zealous about his job. He's related to my sister through her marriage to his (Ketchum's) cousin's brother-in-law, Tag Alder. But relation or not he doesn't care who he arrests and drags to court. I heard he threw his granny in jail for having one too many bluegills in her catch.

"Mornin' Nettie. Boys," Ketchum said as he appeared out of nowhere and stood with hands on hips while he glared at us.

My nephews screamed and threw their fishpoles and bait up in the air.

"Nice day," Ketchum added.

Wanton and Wiley just stared at Ketchum in his spiffy uniform and shiny badge.

"Wow!" said Wanton. "Are you the cops? We can keep the gold can't we?"

"Gold?" Ketchum said.

"Oh, these boys," I chuckled. "We were just going to the creek to, er, fish for gold."

"Yeah," Wiley said. "Gold nuggets!"

"That so?" Ketchum said, looking down at his fingernails.

"Sure," I said. "Babysitting my nephews here and just trying to keep them from burning the woods down. Heh heh."

"Fishing for gold?"

"You betcha," I said.

"With cane fishpoles and buckets of worms?"

"Well, I told 'em you could catch gold by fishing with the pole," I whispered out of the side of my mouth so's the boys didn't hear. "They're city boys and believe anything."

"And you weren't expecting a fish or two to maybe glom onto your, er, gold bait?"

"Well sir, now that you mention it, I did tell the boys that if that did happen, we had to let the fish go right away because it was illegal to fish without a license. But you don't need a license to fish for gold, do you?"

Ketchum frowned and I could tell that I had him there.

"I promise we'll throw any fish back that we might accidentally catch. I'm just keeping these boys busy so's they stay outa trouble," I said.

"You still need a fishing license, girlie," Will said. "You got the fishing gear. I could confiscate it and write you up. I don't think Judge Nightshade would be at all happy to see a Bramble in his courtroom."

Judge Nightshade, who'd been the local judge ever since I could remember, was known for having a small, hard heart. Between him and Ketchum, I was always walking on thin ice. Hizhonor didn't care for us Brambles. Come to think of it, he didn't care for much for anybody, so it was natural to avoid going before him.

"But," said Ketchum with a shrug, "I got three boys of my own—the wife says she has four boys because I never grew up, har har. I know what you're up to Bramble, but I'm not gonna look like some big jerk in front of your nephews there and take away your stuff." He glanced over at Wanton and Wiley who were collecting the worms that had spilled out of the cans. "I know that PR is part of the job, so I'll let you off this time. But you need to find some other way to, ah, fish for gold. Use an old pie pan or something and pretend that way."

I tried not to let Ketchum see how glad I was with the news.

"Okay," I said. "We'll find some other way to, ah, fish for nuggets and keep these two hooligans out of the slammer. Heh heh."

"See that you do," Ketchum said, and just like a whitetail buck, he vanished into the woods.

"Okay boys," I yelled. "We gotta go back to the cabin and get us some other way to fish for gold."

"Aw gee, Aunt Nettie," they both whined.

*  *  *

I found it wasn't much different driving a big septic truck than my regular truck. Just a few more gears, plus the brakes were different and the mirrors were weird, and there's a bunch of gauges that look broke, and some buttons. I tried a few, and the windshield wipers and four-ways came on. There were some levers and a pump switch and other things on it that I didn't have a clue about. And you can't see what's behind you so the rig beeps when you put 'er in reverse, which is what we did when we got the Honey Wagon to the creek. The boys gave me the idea and it seemed like a good one. Made me proud. It was the youngest who said that the Honey Wagon could suck up a zillion gallons of sewage in fifteen minutes. Got me to thinking how if we sucked up some of that creek water, we'd get some fish along with it. Then we'd just go ahead and pump her out on shore and pick out our supper. Of course I promised the boys we'd find us a bunch of gold nuggets and take our loot into the ATV dealership so's Wanton could have his four-wheeler. Maybe when the boys weren't looking, I'd throw a couple of coins around to encourage them.

Once the Honey Wagon was backed up to the creek, we had to get the hose out and push it a ways into the water. My brother'n law didn't clean things up too good after he did his last job and it smelled like a dead skunk in the middle of August. It was Wanton who showed me how to open the sucking thing and turn on the pump. Said he learned about it on *take your kid to work day*. Anyhow, that part went okay—the sucking.

"So what do we do now?" I asked Wanton.

"Dunno," the boy said. "Dad always drives the truck somewhere to dump it. He didn't show me that part because I had lacrosse practice after school. Plus he doesn't dump it every time. I think he goes to some treatment lagoon or something."

"Maybe we should go back to the gravel pit," I said, squinting at the gauges. I looked at the one telling me how full the tank was. It might have been broken though because it was way past full. If it was even half full of fish, we'd have enough to last all winter! I'd maybe slip the boys each a root beer and get them agreeable to learn about cleaning fish. Except the youngest one jumped the gun. Before we could get the hose all back on the truck and head to the gravel pit, Wiley messed with some lever and we heard a loud whooshing sound like when Pickle Dam busted and let go so much water that it filled up the gravel pit and washed away our outhouse.

"Turn it off you dummy!" yelled the older one to his brother.

But Wiley got scared at the gallons of creek water that was pouring out of the hose onto the bank. And it wasn't just creek water. You could see them flushable wipes, like MarshMarigold has in her toilet room, swirling around all over the place in a foamy mess, mixing in with doo-doo and whatnot. It came so fast that I was almost swept off my feet and had to climb a tree. Wanton jumped up onto a truck tire to get out of the way, but Wiley wasn't so lucky and the boy got knocked down into the swirl and was being carried off in the current.

I knew my sister would have my hide if anything happened to her kid, so I scrambled down outa the tree and grabbed the boy. He looked like a mini swamp thing from a late-night movie.

Finally the stuff quit coming and slowed to a trickle. Most went into a ravine next to the woods, some into the creek, and some just oozed around the truck in a sludgy puddle.

Wanton jumped down from the tire he was standing on and started to wade through the goo.

"What are you doing!" Wiley shrieked. He was standing with his arms out, afraid to move. A chunk of something nasty dripped off the back of his head.

"I'm looking for gold nuggets, you dummy," Wanton snarled.

Then Wiley started wailing and calling for his ma. I grabbed him and headed towards the creek to wash him up.

"Hey! Here's one," Wanton yelled.

I drug Wiley over there and looked. It was a bright, shiny fishing lure.

"Good for you, kid. You got something there," I said. Wanton was grinning ear-to-ear.

"Hey! Here's a nugget! Look Aunt Nettie," Wiley squealed.

The boy held up a shiny pebble that was probably quartz. "You're right there kiddo. Looks gold to me."

"Wow!" he said. "Cool."

Wasn't a dang fish to be found, but we had a couple of small ticked off snapping turtles and a bunch of bloodsuckers squirming around in the goop. We dug out a couple of bucks worth of empty beer cans, a flip flop, a busted fishpole, two more lures, three bobbers, a duck decoy head, a wallet (empty), a cap, three socks, a chain from a bicycle, a broken jackknife, and a buck fifty in change that were mostly coins I'd scattered around.

"Let's get to the creek and wash up," I said to the boys, "then we'll see about getting back to the cabin and we won't tell granny about this. We'll just tell her we got skunked fishing." I gave the boys a little wink and nudge to seal the deal.

"Skunked?" Wanton said. "Like sprayed by a skunk?"

"Nope, though we kinda smell like that," I said. "It means we didn't catch any fish. Now get over here and wash up."

We got ourselves rinsed off pretty good and I was just trying to figure out what to tell Ma about how the boys got wet when ol' Ketchum does his magic act and just steps out of the woods and stares at the sludge puddle surrounding the Honey Wagon. He said something bad and started looking around.

"Duck!" I hissed at the boys.

We all pinched our noses and went under for as long as we could. When we come up I hear Ketchum saying more bad words and see him writing down the license plate of the Honey Wagon.

"I know you did this, Bramble," he yelled, looking around. "This here's an environmental disaster!"

Me and the boys ducked back under again and when we popped back up, Ketchum had vanished.

"Wow Aunt Nettie, this was the coolest thing we've ever done!" said the youngest.

"Yeah!" said the oldest. "First we get slimed, then find a bunch of treasure and almost get thrown in prison by the cops! Wait 'til we tell Mom."

"Well, now boys, if we want to

keep having—er, fun, we can't go blabbing to your ma or pa," I said as we all crawled up the steps into the cab of the truck. I got her started and spun the wheels a tad before we could get going.

"I'm thinking 'specially your pa don't need to know we took the truck out for our, um, fishing trip."

"Okay," the boys said, nodding and smiling.

"We all just went cane fishing and come up with nothing but had fun and if Ketchum don't take your pa's truck away, maybe we can try again to get more treasure."

"Awesome," said the oldest. "Can we come over again real soon, Aunt Nettie?"

"Of course," I said. Give me a couple more visits and I'd have two *real boys* for nephews.

We were mostly dry when we clomped into the cabin.

"Ya have you a good time" Ma said. "Where's my catfish?"

The boys give her a good hug and say we got skunked.

Ma give the air a sniff and said, "smells like ya got skunked all right!"

"Nah," said the oldest. "Me and Wiley fell into the creek."

"Just being boys," I said. I was real proud how quick my nephew could spin a tale.

Ma cackled like she does when she's had a little hooch.

"Now go out back at the pump and wash up," she said. "We'll have us some forest stew for supper."

"Oh boy!" yelled my nephews as they raced out the door.

"Forest stew?" I said.

"Sure," Ma said, reaching for her pocketbook. "Here's ten bucks. Go get a pound of hamburger from the likker store. I'll throw in some ruttabeggar and onions."

I took the money and headed for my truck.

"Nettie?"

"Yeah, Ma?"

"Take yer truck, not the Honey Wagon, eh? I 'spect it gets better mileage."

Nothing gets past Ma.

# Roadkill Justice

Let me make this clear, I don't poach.
Not deer, geese, rabbits or even eggs in
boiling water. What I did was an act of
environmental responsibility, even though
the district conservation officer, Will Ketchum,
says otherwise. Ketchum says he caught me red-
handed loading up a deer carcass into the bed of my
truck, which I will point out isn't easy for one gal to do
by herself. Anyhow, it was clear as Lake Superior on a
sunny day that the thing had been mowed over and I know
by who, or whom.

Whatever.

It was them Maki boys, Toivo and Eino, who, *way* after the fact,
claimed the deer was theirs legally since they ran it over. When
Ketchum asked why they didn't call the police to get a roadkill permit,
they hemmed and hawed, saying they was going to, but just didn't get
around to it when they ran home to get a tarp (obviously to cover the
evidence!). Then, says the Makis, when they come back, I was loading
up the deer and 'bout scared them outa their skivvies when I pulled a
gun and told them to back off. Now Will Ketchum and I both know
that those Maki boys didn't call the law for a roadkill permit because
of the large quantity of empties banging around in their piece of junk
truck, which incidentally is no way street-legal, and you could smell the
cheap beer coming off them into the next county. Anyhow, as far as
I'm concerned, roadkill is finders' keepers, even though those Maki
boys say otherwise.

So, CO Ketchum gets all bossy, strutting around writing me up a
ticket for illegal possession of a deer. Something about possession being
nine-tenths of the law, but I guess that is only for persecuting me,

because even though I possessed nine-tenths of the critter (with the other tenth being impossible to scrape up), Ketchum took the carcass for what he called evidence. He did let go the fact that I pulled my shotgun on the Makis, since any gal with half a brain would be looking for the nearest weapon when meeting up with those two bums. What really toasted my marshmallows was that he gave the Makis what he called an appearance ticket and said nothing about them having a few and driving on expired everything under the sun, moon, and stars, including their NRA membership cards. And then the two butt-cheeks were *still* saying it's their deer, and Ketchum says it belongs to the State of Michigan, not none of us. I point out I'm a citizen of the Yooper part of Michigan and got some legal claim to that deer and other critters roaming the forest. Will said not according to the law and then he wrote me up a ticket for illegal possession of the deer, and that far as he was concerned, that we could all "tell it all to the judge."

Which we did.

Judge Nightshade fit his gloomy name perfect. He was pale gray, like he'd never seen the sun, and his chin skin hung in folds over the collar of his black judge's robe in a kind of fleshy waterfall. I wasn't sure what he had perched on his head—it looked like the pelt of a varmint. And a live one at that because it kept creeping forward

making Hizzoner reach up and shove it back up off his forehead.

Anyway.

At first, I laughed when Judge Nightshade reminded Toivo and Eino Maki that he had warned them in the past that he never, *ever* wanted to see their sorry hides in his courtroom again, and that if his (Nightshade's) wife, Rosemary, wasn't a five-times removed cousin of his (Toivo's) wife, Tami, he'd throw the book at them (Toivo and Eino). When I suggested that it seemed all us Yoopers were somehow related and maybe Hizzoner could go easy on a gal just trying to clean up a mess on the highway, Nightshade banged his gavel and told me I was out of order and said, "I'll get to you, young lady." I remember when Ma used to call me young lady, and it didn't bode well.

CO Will Ketchum come out smelling like a fresh-baked pasty and Nightshade told him to dispose of the deer properly. In no uncertain terms would the animal be distributed to any of us who were giving him indigestion and possibly forcing him to consider early retirement. Ketchum said that the carcass was at Tribal Taxidermy being processed and that the meat could go into the foodbank freezer. Since I was a regular customer of the foodbank, I had to smile because I was thinking I might get some of that venison after all.

But I didn't smile for long when ol' Nightshade turned his attention to me.

"Now then, missy, you got caught red-handed with an illegal deer. We can't let that pass, even if it was roadkill. You can of course go to jail for a few days; we got some room in the women's cellblock. Or maybe you got $500 to pay the usual fine? I could order both, but I'll let you do one or the other."

I considered my options, which I thought were kind of harsh. I didn't have two nickels to rub together let alone five-hundred smackeroos, and I couldn't go to jail because of Ma, who would probably burn the cabin down if I wasn't there to keep an eye on her. Or she could go live with my sister, which would be like putting a badger and a tiger in the same pen and telling them to get along. I swallowed hard, trying not to look scared. I could feel the sweat trickle down my back.

"What else you got, yer Honor?" I said, trying to look remorseful and wondering if I should try blackmail. Everyone knew that

Nightshade had a wandering eye. Everyone except his wife. In fact, his eye wasn't the only part of his anatomy that wandered, and I knew some juicy details. But I figured it wasn't the time to pull that ace out of the hole and maybe it would backfire anyhow. I wouldn't put it past Nightshade to legalize the gas chamber just to shut me up.

Hizzoner glared at me over the top of his cheater glasses thinking about what wicked thing to do to me. I figured it was mostly bluster, just to put a show on for the people who hadn't gone in front of him yet; let them shake in their mukluks a little.

"Well," he said, shuffling papers on his bench. "Maybe there is another option." He shuffled some more papers. "Where'd I put that? Sara! Where's the dang paper from those community do-good people?"

A lumpy woman wearing a rumpled black suit scurried up to him and pointed to something on his bench. "That's Citizens for Community Outreach, Your Honor. Right here, um, in front of you."

"Oh yes. Well, Miss, er Bramble," said Nightshade, "it seems you are in luck. You have a third choice! We call it community service. It's for people who are just starting out their life of crime."

I had never considered myself a budding career criminal but thought the idea of some do-good act was better than jail time. I plastered on a smile and tried to look sorry. "So, like do yous want me to shovel the sidewalk in front of the courthouse on my way out?" I asked. "I could even scatter some salt. Maybe help a little old lady like Sara there down the steps and across the street to the liquor store?"

"Oh no," Nightshade said with a sneer. "Says here they need someone to help out at the Gnarly Woods Senior Complex with some kind of thing called..." He put his glasses back on and squinted at the paper. "Sara! What in tarnation is this?"

Sara peered over his shoulder. "Wrinkle Ranch Rock and Roll Prom Bomb, Your Honor."

"What on God's green earth is that all about?"

"It's all in the name, sir. A prom for the old folks, although I find the term wrinkle ranch in poor taste. Anyway, they dance to an oldies band, dress all up in fancy clothes, have a special dinner, drink—a lot. It's at the Gnarly Woods Senior Complex. Remember, Sir? You and your wife went last year and crowned the king and queen. It was actually two queens because—"

"Right, right," he sputtered. "Now I remember. It was ghastly!"

He mumbled something under his breath sounding like "not enough booze in the world," then peered down at me as if I were a glob of pond scum. The side of his mouth twitched.

"Well, Miss Bramble, it seems we've found your redemption."

I was thinking that jail sounded okay. Three meals a day, a nice warm cell, electricity and running water (two things my cabin lacked), and probably a TV in the rec area. Maybe my Perfect Sister could watch out for Ma who would behave herself if you made sure she had her special medicine.

"Well, I was thinking—" I began.

Nightshade slammed his gavel and bellowed, "You should have done your thinking before you loaded up that roadkill. I sentence you to report immediately to, er, Sara, what the hell does this say?"

"I believe it says to report to Miss Figgy, she's the director, and a Bea Righteous, philanthropist."

I wasn't sure what a philanthropist was—maybe somebody who studied fungus or bear scat or something.

"Be there tomorrow morning, at 8:00 a.m.," barked Nightshade.

"Excuse me Your Honor," Sara said. "I know Linda Figgy. She doesn't get there that early. Maybe more like nine-ish?"

The Judge pulled off his glasses and gave Sara a look. "Who's running this courtroom, Sara?"

"Why you, sir, of course," she said, smirking a little as she absently brushed at her skirt. It looked to be covered with some kind of animal hair. Probably cat. She seemed like a cat person.

"Okay, just checking," he said with a sarcastic tone. "NINE-ISH!"

The gavel slammed and I felt a chill run down my spine, as if a cell door had clanged shut on me.

# Prom Bomb

(With a special guest appearance from do-gooder, Miss Bea Righteous)

Nothing but wanton debauchery, if you ask me. Not that anybody did ask me, but I, Bea Righteous, feel compelled to render my opinion. While I did agree to help sponsor a fundraiser for my current residence, the Gnarly Woods Senior Complex, my intentions were nothing but honorable. In spite of the exorbitant monthly rent and fees levied upon Gnarly Woods residents, funds have been lacking for some much-needed upgrades to the complex, including a pond, fountain and gazebo, and, most importantly, a chapel with regular services, which I insisted upon. I presumed, quite wrongly, that the fundraising would be conducted through craft sales or a cake walk or, what I consider my best idea, a Bible scripture recitation contest. Instead, the activity would be a riotous party involving alcohol and rampant licentiousness: the undisputed formula for devilish outcomes.

After all, if you engage a band called the Dirty Devils you must expect nothing less than demonic displays of unabashed exhibitionism and music so raucous it would raise the dead. While I can appreciate the classic older songs, such as one might enjoy on reruns of the Lawrence Welk Show, I don't consider rock and roll gyrations in any way decent or even safe, especially when half the dancers are toting canes, walkers, and portable oxygen machines.

It should in no way be construed that I, Bea Righteous, am aligned with The Evil One, in spite of my uncanny ability to prevail at games of chance. This, I surmise, is due to my iron-clad partnership with the Lord, who opens doors and provides resources along with disciples to accompany me while doing His work.

That said, it was *not* a disciple that was sent my way to assist in the planning and execution of this debacle, which, by the way was dubbed the Wrinkle Ranch Rock and Roll Prom Bomb, or Prom Bomb for short. Assistance, as it were, came with the injection of some backwoods ninny named Nettie Bramble who, having had a run-in with the law, was sentenced to do community service by "helping" with the party. Just what Gnarly Woods needed: a criminal element mixing with inebriated old people who lack most of their faculties!

But my being a loyal servant to the Lord and answering when called, I resigned myself to the fact that Linda Figgy, our activity director whom we usually call Miss Figgy, or Figgy, but rarely Linda, was determined to pull off this bash, complete with raffle tickets and some ludicrous games. Raffle tickets sold for five bucks a pop, or three for ten, and the prize was a trip to Las Vegas, or *sin city*, a place with which I was all too familiar, but only for an exceedingly worthy cause. In spite of my misgivings about the whole thing, I had pledged to match money raised at the event, as long as a chapel was part of the Gnarly Woods Senior Complex upgrade. I was currently flush, as they call it, from inadvertent winnings while partaking in some games of chance—strictly at the direction of the Lord.

So, Miss Figgy introduced me to this Nettle Bramble, who looked even less thrilled than me to be subjected to this assignment. The Bramble woman was dressed as a lumberjack and smelled faintly of woodsmoke and perhaps pork fat, or maybe overripe fish. When we met, we eyed one another suspiciously. Miss Bramble was the epitome of heathenism, if not a sycophant of Satan. And I, of course, am quite the opposite, so, my heavens, what was the Lord thinking? But not being one to judge or question the Lord's command, I extended a warm welcome and made innocuous small talk.

"So, Miss Bramble—" I began but was rudely interrupted.

"Call me Nettie, eh?" she said. "It's really Nettle, but folks always call me Nettie for short."

"Ok, Nettie, and you can call me Bea, which is short for Beatrice. So, *Nettie* what's your affiliation?"

"Well, I mostly keep to myself—me and Ma. We live all snug like in my cabin out on Bramble Road, past the Boulder Plains snowmobile/ORV trail, eh?"

"No, dear, I mean *religious* affiliation."

"Well, I really don't have none. You got any suggestions?" Nettie said.

"Just as I thought," I sniffed. "We'll worry about that later. Now then, tell me what you'd be contributing to the Prom Bomb?"

"Er, well, I can get a discount on beer kegs at Munchies' Party Store. Then there's the Maki boys, Toivo and Eino, who's not speaking to me right now, but they can get stuff from Wisconsin that's cheap. No deposit, eh?"

I sighed. "Perhaps I didn't make myself clear. I mean what type of organizational skills do you have? For example, you could help plan the food, organize the games and prizes, see to the decorations and so on."

The Bramble woman frowned and looked at her boots, which were caked with mud I might add. Then the little twit's face lit up like she had just figured out how to cross her eyes.

"I'm right good at games. Ma always says, 'Now Nettie, don't play games with me.'"

I sighed again. The Lord had sent me a major challenge with this little nincompoop.

"Very good, then. You're in charge of the games and prizes. There's a budget. You'll need to keep receipts and give them Miss Figgy."

"Who?"

"Figgy. The woman who introduced us a few minutes ago? She's over there either talking to herself or into that wicked device clamped to her ear called a Blue Fang. As I'm sure you're aware, or at least should be aware, Miss Figgy is the activity director here at Gnarly Woods."

"Oh, her. She don't like me."

"Of course she *doesn't*," I muttered. Good heavens, such poor grammar. In all fairness, Linda Figgy had an off-putting personality that we all ignored. Unlike myself, she makes no effort to offer gentle, but firm, guidance to the godless Gnarly residents. "Just do your best," I counseled. "Speaking of best, do you, er, have any other clothes? Also, I should mention that we have a free laundry here at the complex, which I'm sure you could use. Oh, and also a tub/shower combo next to the laundry that the staff uses for assisted bathing. You could certainly partake of that as well."

"I don't need help with my washing. That's what the creek is for, eh? Though it is a tad chilly in the winter."

"I'm sure you'll find a nice, hot shower a very wholesome experience. Now then, let's talk about some appropriate activities."

* * *

So, what's wrong with my clothes? I had on my newest flannel shirt and my denim jeans with only a couple of tiny holes. My sister has an 'lectric washing machine, but I steer clear of the contraption. Still, I'd be open to the idea using one if someone would show me how. Maybe Ma could come along one day. I wondered where folks hung their clothes to dry. Maybe we could string a line down the hallway. Anyway, this Bea Righteous woman was a bit snooty, you ask me. She kept looking down at me, even though I was near as tall as her. Some people have a way looking down, even when sitting in a chair. So, anyways, I wanted to just get this court sentence that was passed down by Judge Nightshade over with. All I did was pick up a roadkill deer off the shoulder of the highway and next thing I know, I'm sent to the old folks' home to serve a sentence.

Old people were everywhere, some in better shape than others, but they all had the same blank expression, like they were robots. My ma is old, but she don't act it. Nope, Ma could still swing an axe and fire a shotgun good as when she was younger, if she had a mind to, which she doesn't. But these old people at Gnarly Woods seemed to spend most of their time watching a gigantic TV, and most of them were napping while the TV blared mostly commercials. Bea Righteous seemed perky enough, but she looked like she sucked on a lemon for breakfast. She wore a big ol' cross around her neck and had matching crosses hanging from her ears, and her clothes smelled like moth balls and greasy chicken. The old gal's hair reminded me of a wasp's nest. Same color, too. I bet if a brick dropped on her head, not one hair would move.

So anyways, the fussy gal, Miss Figgy, gave me a list of junk to get at the dollar store for prizes. Righteous had suggested stupid games like checkers and Parcheesi, but I had other ideas. For example, I mentioned to Miss Figgy that maybe having the old farts play beer pong would be fun, but she just give me that look like I'm some kind of poison toadstool.

*  *  *

While I pride myself on tastefulness over flamboyance, I will admit that the place looked quite festive, with balloons and streamers festooned across the dining/community room. In that most of us Gnarlies were used to an 8:00 p.m. bedtime, the party started at 4:30 p.m., with some light refreshments and recorded elevator music. Dinner would come at 5:30 and the games and live band would follow, then the evening would be wrapped up with the raffle drawing. The event was well advertised and open to non-Gnarlies at $25 a person or $40 a couple. Of course, those people didn't arrive until it was fashionably late and barely in time for dinner. Attendees usually included the Budworm mayor and his wife along with other "socially connected" that needed to put a good deed on their resume'.

Most Gnarlies arrived early, after spending several hours trying to trim a few decades off themselves. Attire was a hideous assortment ranging from senior prom to Phantom of the Opera. The local tuxedo store had come a few weeks prior to take orders for the gents who wanted to go black tie. They got a nice senior discount, too. Many had taken advantage of the offer but in spite of their best efforts, an occasional drooping cummerbund, open zipper, or askew bow tie detracted a bit from the desired image shared among the smattering of male residents.

The ladies went all out in poor taste and lack of decorum. Myrtle Gawp, for instance, who had apparently forgotten that she wasn't seventeen anymore, sashayed in with her person mashed into a low-cut glittery sequined gown created for a much younger bosom. A large expanse of wrinkles cascaded down her neck into the sagging abyss of her cleavage, which was cinched severely into place and only managed to stay above her waist through divine intervention.

I, myself, chose a demure black dress with lace shawl that I had worn to Mother's funeral. It fit perfectly, as do all my clothes from my college days when I attended the business school for young ladies. While I don't wear makeup normally—just as I don't drink alcohol (normally)—I did allow for a bit of rouge on my cheeks and small touch of lip gloss.

Miss Figgy really needs to get a full-length mirror, not only for herself, but for her escort, Elwood Fuddy, who's the manager of Gnarly Woods Senior Complex and who rarely leaves the inner sanctums of his office for fear of a Gnarly encounter.

The Figgy/Fuddy combo looked like a bad trip from the 60s, with a hideous display of fringe, white vinyl, enormous lapels, and chest hair. As for revering the 60s, a more decadent time never existed in the history of our country. Free love, flower power, open marriage, the rise of atheism, sit-ins, drugs, and dreadful, suggestive music. I was glad that our Prom Bomb band, The Dirty Devils, promised to play classically clean music that even the Pope would approve of. Indeed! The Pope would certainly *not* have approved. But I digress...

* * *

Everyone did clean up pretty good, and they all seemed perked up, too. There was some fancy wine along with beer and soda pop on a drink table, and lots of little goat-turd sized bites of stuff that mostly tasted like they looked. I took a couple of beers for Ma and me but got the evil eye from both Figgy and Righteous, so I pretended to put one back, but didn't. I popped the top for Ma and she took a swig. A little dribbled out the sides of her mouth because she's missing a couple of teeth—well more than a couple—and had that hair lip when she was born, which they sewed up, but not very good. Anyway, between the two afflictions, she did sometimes have some leakage. Ma had gone to the thrift store and bought me and her a couple of fancy dresses. Ma can sew and she did some adjustments, and I thought we looked pretty good. Damn sexy, truth be told. I guess we did look hot and this fella named Hector Paine who rode around on an 'lectric scooter tooled up to Ma and asked her to dance.

"Well, you old fart," Ma said, "how do ya reckon we can do that with you in that contraption?"

"Hop aboard woman! I'll show ya," ol' Hector said.

"Dance band ain't started yet," Ma said.

"That doesn't matter, my dear!" Hector said. "We'll make our own music."

I had been around long enough to know a "line" when I heard one. But, like I said, Ma don't act her age and she pulled up her long dress, with the added slit up the side, and plunked right into the old geezer's lap and off they go, whirring around in circles.

I saw crabby Bea Righteous standing all by herself so I go over to her and try to talk. She sees the beer I'm hiding and does one of those eyebrow arch things. Except I notice that she's got a glass of wine, so, I give it right back.

"It's important to fit in," Bea said, "so I do have a little sip or two of wine, even though alcohol is a slippery slope to the Evil One's lair."

Whoa! If it was, half of the county would be goners. I didn't know much in the religion department, but I did know that God was up and Satan was down. I always wondered why folks bowed their heads *down* to pray, since *up* was where the prayer was headed. I also wondered about this virgin stuff that was always cropping up. I asked Ma about it and she sent me to a church down the street to go to Sunday school and "ask them yer dumb questions." The teacher said I was the first child to be expelled from Sunday School for inappropriate behavior. That was the end of my religious learning.

So anyways, people started sitting at tables because it was time for dinner. Me and Bea and Figgy and Fuddy all sat at one table. Ma was off with that old prune driving the scooter. Pretty soon we got served plates of food that wouldn't keep a starving cur dog happy. There was some little white lump of meat, two tiny spuds, a few cooked carrots, and a hunk of green stuff that I guess was to fill an empty spot on the plate. I took a bite of the meat, which might have been chicken. It was cold and like chewing a boot heel. Good thing that I'd filled up on the goat turd snacks earlier. I was getting a little nervous about when dinner was over because next came the games I'd planned and there were so many old people who'd had more than a few. I wondered how they'd handle the balloon contest.

* * *

Chicken again. Or at least I assumed that's what the rubbery little disc was on my plate. We Gnarlies all knew if we didn't eat what was on our plate, that it would be recycled into the next day's meal, so we either forced ourselves to eat it, or we "accidentally" dropped it onto the floor with the hopes they wouldn't scrape it off and salvage it.

Figgy strutted up to the makeshift stage where a microphone was set up. Directly in front of the stage area sat several plastic totes, awaiting the revelation of the fun to come.

"Okay everyone. Go ahead and finish up your cake and then we need to shove the tables along the walls and have you all come up front and Miss Nettie Bramble will get the games going."

There was a single cheer and whistle from the crowd, presumably from the hag that Nettie called "Ma." Everyone else groaned. We Gnarlies had been subjected to so many childish activities during our tenure at the complex, that we all felt as if we'd reverted back to kindergarten.

Nettie clomped up to the stage area. I noticed she had boots under her droopy gown, which she failed to fill out.

"Okay yous come up and we got a balloon game. Menfolk here and ladies here," said Nettie. "Ma, you come on up and demonstrate."

Well, my heavens, the object of the game was for the woman to hold a balloon behind her back and the man was supposed to come up and pop it while thrusting himself at the backside of the woman. As you can imagine, it was reprehensible! The first balloon to succumb to the pounding and pop would announce the winners, who would choose some cheesy prizes from one of the totes. It was interesting to me how Hector Paine managed to easily get off his scooter and attack "Ma" from the rear with wild abandon. And even though employees were not allowed to take any prizes, Miss Figgy and Mr. Fuddy were fully participating, though not properly, as they had chosen to face one another, and even though their balloon slipped away, they continued to gyrate rather unabashedly. I, myself, chose not to join in and was waiting to see who had the first heart attack.

* * *

Well, if that didn't liven things up. Folks were doubled over laughing trying to get their balloons to pop, or maybe they were gasping for breath. Whatever, they had smiles on their faces instead of looking like a box of glazed donuts. There weren't enough men to go around, and those that we had were slowing down and quitting, forcing two gals to do the deed, which was a real hoot. After a while, most gave up and there was just two couples left, with Ma and the scooter guy, Hector, among them. Folks formed a circle around the two couples, egging 'em on, until Ma and Hector popped their balloon first. Everyone cheered like it was the Olympics. Hector staggered back to his scooter and he and Ma went and picked themselves out a couple of beer cozies from the prize tote tub.

* * *

I must say I was relieved when the games blessedly ended and the band came on stage. I mean that Bramble woman—what was she thinking? After that ludicrous balloon popping contest, they had a relay competition with Life Saver candy on a toothpick held in the mouth. Firstly, many of the Gnarlies have gaps in their teeth, or false teeth, or just plain gums, which makes holding a toothpick in one's mouth difficult, although I was told that strong lips were an asset. Then passing a piece of candy down the line like that. My Heavens! A germ-a-rama nightmare. Then there was passing along a tennis ball chucked under one's chin. While the extra neck wrinkles made this game feasible, one could not ignore the likelihood of rampant Covid and flu viruses.

There was a horrible squealing from the leader of the band as he blathered into the microphone *check-check-check-check-check* until the residents began throwing food at him. (A lot of food had made its way to the floor.) While I was waiting for a nice piece of dance music to temper the unruly crowd, I noticed a party crasher. Well, not really crasher, because the public was invited, but they needed to sign up beforehand so that we could reject such deplorables as the town drunk, village idiot, and drain commissioner. Clearly, this man who arrived alone and smartly dressed in a crisp, black tuxedo, was not from Budworm. His hair was so black it gleamed indigo highlights. He had a little pointy beard, perfectly trimmed and a peek of red showing just above his top jacket button. I reached up and patted my hair, which of course was perfectly in place. I decided that it didn't hurt to lose the shawl and expose a couple of inches of neckline, which I will point out, was still fairly firm. Swan neck they had called me in school. It was one of my best features Mother always said. My horrid twin sisters, Ida and Iva, called me swamp neck. Their jealousy was so transparent.

\* \* \*

The band was hot! They started out with a good one that *everybody* knew: The "Hokey Pokey." Trouble was, it kind of turned into a striptease act. When folks were putting their foot in and out and shakin' all about, the gals all pretty much kicked off their shoes and tossed their shawls and whatnot every which way. One or two even peeled out of their girdles and stockings. Then went the men's jackets, cummerbunds, suspenders, belts, and one fella took off his shirt and whirled it over his head and winged it up on stage. When we put our whole selves in and our whole selves out then shook it all about, a few of the fellas lost their pants: one boxer and one brief and one who forgot his underdrawers.

Then this ol' gal whose bosom had nearly popped out sidled up to me and jabbed me with her elbow. She said her name was Myrtle Gawp and she wondered who the hottie was with ol' pruneface. Pruneface being Bea Righteous who, sure enough had a good looking fella talking to her.

Well, the "Hokey Pokey" ended and the band was playing a slow dance. Folks put some of their clothes back on and coupled up as best you can when there's four gals to every guy. Then Righteous and Mr. Hot Stuff sashay out on the floor and start some kind of floaty dance while the band guy at the microphone sang "Could I Have this Dance for the Rest of My Life?" He was out of tune, too. The old folks liked it, though. Even Ma, who don't admit she's older'n dirt, got into it with the scooter dude. I wondered when his battery would poop out.

\* \* \*

"My name's Sebastian Baskerville," said the party crasher to me as we waltzed around the dance floor. My heavens, but he was a divine dancer. I felt that we were perhaps dancing a little too close but decided that it would be rude to pull away. I was quite pleased with myself for remembering the waltz, which I learned along with other classic dance steps as an elective course at the business school for young ladies that I attended back in my youth.

"Bea Righteous," I responded, my voice feeling a little thick.

"Ah, but it's so much more *fun* to be a little sinful, don't you think?"

"Righteous is my name," I sniffed, perhaps pulling away just a hair.

"But not your game?" he said, perhaps pulling me a little closer.

"I don't play games," I responded rather tersely.

"Yes, I agree," he said, twirling me around. "Games are tedious."

"So, Mr. Baskerville—"

"Friends call me Seb—short for Sebastian, which is a ridiculous family name I inherited."

The waltz ended and a polka started. We looked at each other and made our way to a table along the edge and sat.

"Okay—Seb—what brings you to this affair? I don't recall seeing you at any of our other fundraisers."

"Well, I'm new around here and thought this sounded like a good opportunity to scout for some new, er get to know the community—a fundraiser and all. I see there is a raffle."

"Yes indeed. Unfortunately, I do not believe that the prize is appropriate."

"Oh?" he said, arching a perfectly pointy eyebrow at me.

I noticed for the first time that his eyes—those eyes—were beyond brown and so dark they were nearly black and were like gazing into a mysterious abyss. I quickly averted my gaze lest my intentions be misunderstood.

"Yes. A trip to Las Vegas," I said clucking my tongue. "I mean, why not Branson or Graceland or Dollywood? Why Sin City?"

I will admit that this statement was a bit hypocritical in that I had, myself, done a bit of gambling, but only as a short-term investment maneuver to (mostly) benefit the Budworm Methodist Church Camp For Wayward Youth that needed a new lodge.

"Well, Vegas is fun," he replied. "Truthfully, it's kind of my home base. A lot of potential quarry, er, opportunities there for me. While most people go to Vegas on vacation, I *leave* to get away."

I peered at him over the rims of my glasses. "Indeed. Are you a professional gambler?"

"I guess you could say that, though I do have a great interest in the human soul."

"I see, well that is honorable," I conceded.

There was an ear-piercing squeal from the microphone. We looked up to see Figgy fiddling with it.

"Okay Ladies and Gents!" she screeched. "Time for the big drawing!"

The band's drummer did a dramatic drum roll and a cymbal crash. A smattering of applause followed.

Crisco Motley, the Gnarly Woods handyman, wheeled out the revolving cage that we used on bingo night. He stood grinning on stage, running his hand over his slicked-back hair.

"You may leave now," Figgy said to Crisco, who shuffled off the stage muttering to himself.

"Now, then, could I please have someone who does *not* have a raffle ticket come up on stage?"

We all looked around. Admittedly, I had purchased the three for ten, just to be supportive of the cause.

"I would be honored to select the winner," said Sebastian, standing and making a small bow toward Figgy.

"Oh my," Figgy said, patting her faux red curly hair. "And who is this?"

"Sebastian Baskerville at your service, Madam," he said with another little bow.

"SPIN THE DAMN THING AND PICK ME," shouted someone from the crowd. Of course, it was Myrtle Gawp, who had at least hitched her bodice back up to a decent height.

"I will do my best," responded Seb.

"AND THEN YOU AND ME CAN HOT FOOT IT TO SIN CITY! I MIGHT BE OLD BUT I CAN TEACH YOU A THING OR—"

"That's quite enough, Myrtle. Take your seat," Figgy said. She spun the basket vigorously and it coasted to a stop. "Mr. Baskerville, if you please."

He pulled out a ticket and handed it to Figgy.

"And the winner of an all-expense paid trip for two to Fabulous Las Vegas is..."

\* \* \*

The handsome dude on stage was old enough to be my uncle, but he sure had a way about him that heated me up pretty good. Since I was a party planner, I couldn't enter the contest, but Ma did. Me and her would have a blast at Vegas. We'd been to the Indian casino and done some gambling, and Ma was pretty lucky. Me, well, I might as well throw my quarters out the window on the way and save me some time.

"Beatrice Righteous!" announced Mr. Hottie.

Ol' Bea gave out a little chirp from over at the side and made her way up to the stage to have her pitcher taken and all.

The handsome dude gave her a smack-a-roo right on the lips and presented her with a certificate of some kind. Oh well, I didn't much like the idea of flying anyway. Probably they cheaped out on the seats and you had to ride back with the suitcases and all.

\* \* \*

My Heavens! I hadn't been kissed by a non-related man for, well, maybe back in sixth grade when Billy Doodle kissed me, against my will, on a bet. He also ate worms and drank fake blood (unsweetened red Kool Aid) on a bet. Anyway, it took me aback—Seb's kissing me *on the lips*—but I knew that lust was one of the fourteen deadly sins, and it ranked pretty high on the worst-sin list, so I demurely took the certificate from his well-manicured hand. I admit it made me feel posh when he took my elbow and escorted me off stage while some of the losers clapped for me. The band started some horrific rock and roll nonsense and the off-key lead singer screamed into the microphone, "JITTERBUG!" And off went everyone trying to do a dance that was meant for teenagers. It would be a miracle from God if we made it through the evening without a stroke, heart attack, or broken hip.

Seb and I sat and watched the gyrating mass. Then he suggested that we might be on the same flight to Vegas and I was welcome to use his travel agent. He asked who I might take. Or perhaps he could be my plus one.

Indeed! Such impropriety. Yet it was only a plane ride and going together would reduce the chance of my being ensconced between two screaming, runny-nosed youth. And I do believe that where God leads one must follow even into the jaws of, well, heck. For some unfathomable reason, the Good Lord keeps sending me to Vegas. This time with a disciple. All I can do is obey.

# Cross Wired

See, Ma, she couldn't read the letter because she never went to school. "That's what I gots you around for," she'd say. Ma was always sure to point out my shortcomings, such as being a lousy cook and overall lazy, which was a hoot since she hardly got out of her chair. She did it just to keep me in my place so's I didn't get all snooty about going to school (fairly regular) and getting a diploma.

So anyway, this letter comes and it was from the Northern Electric Co-op, which was a puzzle, since we didn't have 'lectricity at the cabin because we're too far out in the sticks. In fact, our mailbox is three miles down the two-track we live on that doesn't even have a street sign, but everyone calls Bramble Road.

So, even though I could read, I wasn't real quick to understand what the Co-op was blabbing on about with all their fancy language about the electrification of rural areas and how we could get wired up with no cost if we could prove need.

"We ain't got no need," Ma said. "Kerosene has done us fine for this long, no reason to change."

Since I may have skipped school from time to time, I maybe missed out on how to understand fancy writing, I asked MarshMarigold (I like to call her M&M, which ticks her off) and her ornery ol' man, Tag, to come and tell us what it was about.

"Well," Tag said, "it's not that hard to figure out. You're all living like a bunch of bush colts out here what with no electricity or indoor plumbing, and they want to at least get you electrified. Wouldn't hurt to have a well put in and get some running water."

"Hand pump works fine," Ma snapped.

"Except in the winter," I snapped back.

"So yous got to heat a little water to thaw her out. Don't kill you," Ma said.

"Sure, old woman, while you sleep in, I do all the damn work," I said.

M&M piped up, "Ma, tag and I have said all along you can live in the apartment above the garage. Lots of room for you"

MarshMarigold gave me a beady look. Clear as day that I wasn't being offered a cozy place above the garage.

"Phooey!" Ma said. "What the hell would I want to do that for? Me and Nettie do fine here."

"Hah!" I said.

"ANYWAY," Tag said. "Says here they will hook you up to electricity at no cost. Of course we'd have to wire the cabin. Put in some light figures. It wouldn't take much."

"You drive a septic truck," I said. "What you know about wiring?"

"I've learned a few things," he said. "I got the Man Gene and I just naturally can do wiring and plumbing and such. It's born in me. Just like cooking and cleaning is born in you gals, along with raising kids."

Me, Ma, and M&M all snorted at the same time. None of us could cook much or cared to, and cleaning was a big waste of time. And so far the jury was out on raising kids, with Wanton and Wiley being such sissy pants.

"I think you might wanna do this," Tag said, "because they may come after you for zoning violations."

"Zoomin' whaaa?" I said.

"Zoning," Tag said. "You're supposed to have electricity, a flush toilet and whatnot according to the township. You're grandfathered in, Mother Bramble, but Nettie here probably isn't. You could be going against the law and have to go to court."

I wasn't sure how my sewer sucking brother-in-law was reading all that into a letter from the 'lectric company and what my grandfather— who I never met—had to do with it, but I also knew that I didn't want to go before Judge Nightshade again anytime soon.

Well, Ma had been enjoying some of her medicinal whiskey and nodded off after mumbling that she didn't care what we did because she was gonna die soon anyway.

"Probably outlive us all," said MarshMarigold.

"Sure," said Tag, "she's so pickled that she'll be preserved forever."

Having the cabin 'lectrified seemed like a good idea to me, so me and M&M filled out the papers and put them in the return envelope and she promised to put on a stamp and mail it.

Well, before you know it, a big ol' truck with a bucket attached to a long kind of arm thing came along and strung a wire from the highway down Bramble Road. They even cleared out a bunch of the brush and trees and made the road real nice. Next they planted a big pole in the yard and run a wire up to the side of the cabin. Then they left.

That's when the trouble all started—when my stupid and cheap brother'n law decided not to hire a real 'lectrician because him and his Man Gene could take care of it. He ends up going to some hardware store with a fancy name of "Thadwell's Repurpose Depot" and picks up a bunch of used junk that he calls "previously enjoyed."

Then things got worse when Tag bought a book called *Wiring for Dumbbells* and started drilling holes in the walls and yanking through wire here and there while M&M read from the book, her face all scrunched up.

"Say's here," she said, "that the black is hot and the white is neutral and the green or bare copper is ground."

"I know that, but what about a blue wire. The guy at the hardware said I needed blue for the three-way switch," he said, sweat popping out on his brow.

"No, you're supposed to have yellow for a three-way. What in heck do they need a three- way switch for anyway?" M&M said.

"So's they don't have to across the living room to flick on the light," Tag said.

The living room only took about ten steps from one side to the other, but I knew to keep my trap shut. Ma on the other hand...

"Typical man," Ma said, as she awoke from her boozy nap. "Won't ask fer directions and tries to do something he's got no right doin'. Yer gonna burn the place down!"

"Now Mother," said M&M, "Tag is real handy. He fixed my washer."

I happened to know that when Tag fixed the washer that it not only *wasn't* fixed, but when it went into the spin cycle, it did the mambo across the utility room floor, out the door, and down the steps before it crashed and busted up in the back yard, scaring the bejesus out of the neighbor's dog that was taking a nap under a nearby tree.

"Never mind about all these extra wires. Now give me that light fixture..."

After a couple of days, me and Ma lost interest and just let the two Bickersons drill, pull, hang, and cuss. At one point, their two boys, Wanton and Wiley, come along to supposedly learn a thing or two from their pa, but they got bored and asked if they could go play in the woods. We warned them not to start any fires, chop down any trees, kill any critters, or thump on each other.

"Aw gee," Wanton said. "What else is there?"

"Take a pole and go on down to the river and see if you can catch us some fish for supper," I said.

"I'm not digging up worms!" Wiley said.

"Use the stale marshmallows in the cupboard," Ma said. "Now git!"

A couple of hours after the boys thundered out of the cabin, Tag stood up from the outlet where he'd been working and dusted hisself off then does a few arm stretches to get the kinks out and probably show off some man muscles, if he had any. "She's all done!" he said.

"She is?" said M&M.

"Sure, just gotta throw the main circuit breaker on and we are in business," he said. "Just think, Ma, you can have a refrigerator to keep stuff cold. I'll check out the used appliance store tomorrow. And I even installed a doorbell outside the cabin door."

"Well, now I wouldn't mind having a cold beer once in a while," Ma said, warming up a little to her son-in-law, "but I don't know what I need a doorbell for. We can hear people coming a mile away rattling down Bramble Road."

"Okay, here goes!" Tag said as he disappeared into the back closet of the kitchen where he had rigged up a box that he'd run the 'lectric through.

"THREE, TWO, ONE!" he hollered from the back. "CONTACT!"
Nothing.

"What the?" he said. "Oh, maybe if I—"

Then there was a snap, crackle, and sizzle and ol' Tag let out a yelp. The light didn't come on but the doorbell took to buzzing like crazy.

Tag ran out into the living room and looked like he'd been caught up in a tornado, what with his hair sticking straight up. He was holding his hand and jumping around like he had a squirrel up his trousers, and he was missing one shoe and sock. I guess his Man Gene took a vacation because he sure had screwed things up.

"Tag, honey, are you okay?" said MarshMarigold as she rushed to him.

"Arggg, ald fooey doughty wampa!" he said.

"Where's my cold beer?" Ma said.

The doorbell stopped buzzing and the light in the living room came on real bright, then dim then bright and dim and kept doing it. Wanton and Wiley burst in, dragging along a snapping turtle glommed onto a fishing line.

"We pushed the doorbell!" yelled the older one. "And a couple of sparks came out."

"Yeah! It was cool," said the younger one.

Just then the living room light let out a pop and died. The doorbell started to buzz on and off, then kind of faded and died.

"Wabba dimma doodle!" blubbered Tag.

"Tag! The children. No cussing!" said M&M.

"I'd settle for a warm beer," Ma said.

"We caught a fish!" said the youngest.

"Can we eat him?" said the oldest.

I looked at the snapper. It looked pretty ticked off, then made a jerking motion and spit out the hook still baited with a chunk of stale marshmallow. Then ol' snappy, probably looking to get even for being dragged around by a couple of hooligans, starts a journey across the living room, heading for Tag.

"Waaza! Pizzpewee!"

I had heard about folks speaking on what was called "tongues," which I guess is a way to talk to the Lord, so's only He can understand. I wondered if that was what Tag was doin'. I figured he got some kind of special power when he 'lectrocuted hisself.

That's when snappy decided that Tag's toe on the bare foot looked pretty good, so he grabbed on and wasn't gonna let go.

"Someone bring me my sipping whiskey!" Ma barked.

I ignored her because I was enjoying the dance that Tag and the turtle was doing all over the living room, his wife screaming all the while that we needed to do something.

That's when we smelled smoke.

"Wow!" said the oldest. "Look! That thing on the pole outside's burning."

It sure was. Big flames shooting above the trees that you could probably see from the next county.

"Sirens!" shouted the youngest. "Way cool! I want to be a fireman when I grow up!"

The fire trucks got there in no time at all, and good thing, since now there was a couple of trees ablaze along with some bramble bushes and our chicken coop. Luckily, we didn't have any chickens.

"I *told* you that the ground wire wasn't optional!" screeched my Perfect Sister.

The snapping turtle finally gave up on Tag's toe and let loose then clambered toward the open door. Two firemen, all duded up in suits, helmets, and boots opened the door then stepped aside to let the turtle pass.

"Fire's all out, folks," said one of the firemen, except it was a gal's voice—a gal fireman!

"We thank you," said MarshMarigold. "It seems that we got our wires crossed here," she said, glaring at her husband who was holding his toe. It didn't seem to be bleeding.

"You boys want a beer?" Ma said to the fireman and firegal.

"No thank you, ma'am. If you folks are gonna do an insurance claim, just get in touch with the township for a report."

"Insurance claim?" I said.

"Sure. Faulty wiring. Happens all the time," said the firegal. She looked around. "Looks like you've got some damage. Insurance should fix things up. But I'm not an expert."

Ma had fallen asleep. The Alder clan left with Tag still speaking in tongues. I went into the bedroom and got the box under the bed that had our valuables like the family Bible, some silver dollars, Ma's old set of fake teeth, and a few papers. Sure enough, there it was, our insurance policy that Tag had sold when he was in the insurance business—before he got into sewer sucking. I remembered paying up for five years, and that was only a couple of years ago.

"Well, I'll be darned," I said. "Maybe we'll get 'lectric after all."

# Left Dangling

Deer season comes with a batch of problems. First off, anyone who knows me knows I got no use for hunting licenses that cost a bundle and far as I can tell, does nothing to help me shoot better or help me find my way out of the woods when I mighta' taken a wrong turn.

So, not having a license can cause me some grief mainly because our conservation officer, Will Ketchum, doesn't take kindly to folks (distant kin or not) wandering around the woods loaded for bear or deer or even birds without an official license. I wish he would get more distant, like into the next county, so's that I didn't have to worry about him popping out of nowhere and scaring the bejesus out of me.

Then comes along my other problem: my relations. MarshMarigold and Tag are always trying to pawn their boys off on me and Ma. It's not the boys' fault, but they're a couple of city sissies and a chore to have around. The latest excuse for dumping the two on us is that the oldest one had a school assignment to come up with a story that had to do with the "culture" of the U.P. and it could be written out, done by taking pitchers, or doing a video, which I guess you can do with a cell phone. Meanwhile Ma thinks I should show my nephews about deer season. I'd poke my eye out before I'd turn over even a BB gun to my nephews. But my Perfect Sister pointed out that Tag was likely to do more harm than good if he tried to show the boys anything besides how to pop open a beer can.

Turns out my nephews would give me just the cover I needed for visiting my tree blind, which CO Ketchum was bound to be sniffing out. He'd have a hard time of it, though because I had it so deep in the woods that even the Good Lord wouldn't see it.

"Now don't lose my phone!" said M&M who gave her fancy phone with the little TV screen on it to Wanton to use for his school project. He was supposed to take nature pitchers with it, or maybe a movie if we saw a deer or bear or something more exciting than a squirrel.

"How come I can't have a phone!" Wiley whined.

"Because you don't have a school project, but your brother needs to share and maybe let you take a photo or two. Maybe Aunt Nettie will shoot a deer and you can get a picture of her posing over the carcass."

"Eeeeeewwww!" shrieked the youngest.

"No no no!" I said. "Nobody is taking my pitcher with my kill."

"How come?" said the oldest.

"Yeah," said M&M, giving me a smirk. "How come?"

"It's a secret is how come. Now do you want me to take these two brats off your hands or not?"

That gave her something to think about.

"No pictures of any dead deer!" she said.

Then the youngest pipes up. "My science teacher says that we shouldn't eat meat because cow farts are messing up the air. Do deer fart too?"

"That's a real good question," Ma piped up. "I 'spect it depends on what they's eatin'."

"Well, my deer should be eating the pile of apples and carrots I left out last week," I said.

"I don't think of them things as making ya fart," Ma said. "Fetch me a beer, Tag."

My Perfect Sister's other half, Tag, had been ignoring the conversation until he heard the word beer. Ma had a nice stash in the new/used fridge that we'd got after the 'lectricity was put in the cabin.

"Sure thing, Mother Bramble," Tag said.

When he got back he had two beers, one for Ma and one for him, like me and my sister don't get thirsty.

"Open 'er up," Ma said. "I got the 'thritis in my hands pretty bad today."

"Sure thing," said Tag as he struggled with the pop top. "What's wrong with this damn thing?" he muttered as he tried to get the little tab pushed back.

"Watch your language," M&M said. "And give me the damn can, you moron."

"Lord almighty," Ma said. "Man can't even open a beer."

"Let's go boys," I said, "before your pa hurts hisself."

Me and the boys piled into my truck. I had my shotgun stashed behind the seat along with some cracklins, deer jerky, and Cokes. I turned the truck key a half dozen times then she fired up and we bumped down Bramble Road and turned off on a goat path that was good and hid in the woods so that even CO Will Ketchum couldn't see it. We bounced along the ruts for a couple of miles then turned at the witch's tree and into a clearing. (Tree's dead and all gnarled up like a witch).

"Well, here we are boys," I announced. "Isn't this a great spot?"

They took a gander at the area and looked at me.

"A great spot for what?" said the oldest.

"This here's my hunting spot," I said.

"Where are we?" said the youngest.

"I told you. My hunting—"

"Are there Bigfoots here?" said the oldest. "I could get an A for sure on my project if I get a picture of a Bigfoot. That would be totally awesome!"

"Yeah!" chimed in the youngest. "Totally cool!"

We all piled out of the truck and I went over to check my bait pile with the boys at my heels. For sure something had been chowing down. I was hoping maybe a six or eight pointer. I didn't shoot the does or spikes. I had my standards.

"PEEEEEYUUUUUU, what smells?" said the youngest.

"You, butt face," snipped his brother. "You stink!"

"Not as much as you. You stink more!"

"You stink so bad that you made a skunk pass out from the smell!"

"Oh yeah? Well you—"

"Well, well, well," came a voice from the woods that made us about jump outa our skin. "What have we here?"

Will Ketchum, plain as day, materializes out of the shrubs like a ghost.

"Morning Nettie, boys."

Darned if that rascal hadn't found my spot.

"I don't suppose you bought your hunting license this year, did you Nettie?" Ketchum said.

"What would I do that for?" I said. "I'm not huntin.' "

Then the youngest opened his trap. "But you said you'd teach us to hunt deer!"

"No, no," I said. "See, I said, I um..."

"I thought we were looking for Bigfoots!" said the oldest.

"Sure, heh heh, Bigfoots," I said trying to give a little wink at Will so's he knew I didn't believe in Bigfoots but was humoring the boys.

"That so?" said Will. "And this here tree stand?"

"What tree stand?" I said.

"This tree stand," he said, pointing to the wooden ladder leading up a big oak tree trunk to a platform, "that overlooks the bait pile."

"Oh *that*," I said. "It's a treehouse for the boys. It was a tree *stand* once, but now I fixed it into a treehouse to surprise the boys."

"Yay!" shouted the boys as they headed toward the ladder. "A treehouse!"

"Dad tried to build us one," said the oldest, "but he fell through the floor and Mom said would have broke his neck if he hadn't been drunk."

"Thanks Aunt Nettie!" said the youngest.

"Now hold on, boys. I'm not so sure that's really a treehouse. Sure looks like a hunting tree stand to me. And I don't suppose you know how this bait pile got here."

"It stinks to high heaven!" shouted the youngest.

"You stink more," said the oldest.

"Do not."

"Do too."

"Knock it off," I snapped.

"You've explained how a hunting tree stand is a treehouse. Now how do you explain the bait pile that I suppose you will say isn't a bait pile," said Ketchum.

"Well, in a way, it is," I said, trying to think up something quick.

"To hunt over from the, er, treehouse, for ..."

"Bigfoots!" said the oldest. "I got a school project."

"Funny how a Bigfoot likes deer bait," said Ketchum.

"Well, see, I know the deer like the apples and carrots," I said, "and your Bigfoots like to eat deer, so it's kind of a double bait pile. I added a wink and nudged Will in the ribs. Pretty hard."

"Ow! That hurt Bramble. Okay, so the boys are looking for a Bigfoot?"

"Right," I said. "And we're going up in the treehouse to watch for the deer to come, and then the Bigfoot will come and Wanton, here, will get a pitcher or maybe a movie on his ma's phone and get an A in school."

"That so," said Ketchum, rubbing his ribs.

"Yup," I said, then sidled up to Will and talked low. "See the boys ma and pa aren't getting along too good and I'm trying to help out by taking the kids off their hands for a spell."

I wasn't sure he was buying it, but he let out a big sigh, like he was giving up. "So, don't expect I'd find a gun or anything like that in your truck?" he said.

"It's behind the seat!" said the blabbermouth youngest.

Will lifted one eyebrow at me. I wasn't sure how he could do that. It didn't seem normal.

"I keep my gun in the truck in case we come across a bear. I gotta protect the boys," I said.

"Sure, sure," said Will, looking up at the deer stand I was calling a treehouse, even though there wasn't actually a house, just a platform. I didn't bother with rails because I had rigged up a harness to attach around me in case the kick from my shotgun set me off balance.

"So, let's take a look at this treehouse," said Will.

"Yay!" shouted the boys as they scurried up the wooden ladder.

"Be careful you two grubs. You fall and break your neck and your ma will kill me."

After a lot of huffing and puffing by Ketchum, who was last up the ladder and maybe getting a little pudgy, we all stood on the platform and looked around.

"Me and the boys was gonna sit up here and eat our lunch and wait for deer, and then the Bigfoot and Wanton here would snap a pitcher. I got some cracklins and Cokes. Plenty if you want some."

"What's cracking?" Ketchum said.

"*Cracklins,*" I said. "It's pig skin and fat all fried up crisp. Ma's specialty outside of her ruttabegger pasties." I pulled a piece out of a stained paper sack and handed it to him.

He took a bit and chewed. "A little chewy, but tasty," he said.

Me and the boys nibbled on ours and everyone had greasy fingers and lips.

"So, just for the record," Ketchum said, "I know this here is a hunting tree stand. I've had my eye on it for a couple of months. Too bad you don't go with the law and get a hunting license like everyone else. Also, I'm very disappointed that you and the boys aren't wearing a speck of blaze orange. I'd hate for you to go before Judge Nightshade again. I hear his hemorrhoids are acting up and that he's real cranky these days."

I didn't take much to the idea of ever facing ol' Nightshade again, since he didn't care much for us Brambles, especially me. "Far as I know, there's no law says you need a license for taking pitchers for a kid's school project," I said kind of snippy. No way was I going to be caught dead in blaze orange. Might as well have a flashing sign showing where me and my huntin' spot are at.

"Sure," said Ketchum, wiping cracklin grease on his pants. "Anyway, long as we're up here in the stand—er, treehouse, I'll show the boys some safety tips. Don't suppose you have a safety harness up here?"

"Yup," I said. "Right behind you."

He turned and picked up a rope—maybe a little frayed—with a big old horse harness strap hooked to the end.

"This is it?" he said.

"Works fine," I said.

"Anyway, fellas, hook yourself up before you do anything," said Ketchum as he strapped the cracked leather strap around his waist. It didn't want to fit, but he cinched it tight, making his eyes pop out a little. "This way, if you fall, the safety harness will catch you."

"Cool!" said the oldest. "Like in the school play we did about Peter Pan where Lubby Luppinen got to fly around. Except he got hurt when he smacked into the wall."

I passed around the Cokes and tried to figure out a way to get rid of Ketchum. All the messing around was sure to keep the deer away, plus I needed to get my gun out of the truck.

"So, officer, me and the boys sure have enjoyed our little visit but I bet yous got a lot of crime to solve out in the woods, so—"

Just then, a big buck, with a rack that musta been a ten-pointer stepped out of the woods. Just my luck that my gun was in the truck and Ketchum was in my tree stand. The buck stood stock-still like it was posing for a good shot, except the only shot would be with that phone camera.

"Wanton," I hissed, "get a pitcher."

We all moved around real quiet while Wanton gets the phone pointed at the big ol' boy.

"This is probably killing you, eh Bramble," Ketchum said with a sneer.

"I don't know what yous are blabbing about," I said maybe just a little too loud because the buck spooked and darted away.

Except it wasn't me that spooked it.

"Look!" shouted Wiley, "It's a Bigfoot coming!"

We all turned to look, but didn't see a Bigfoot, because there's no such thing. Except it was something making the trees move and crackin' branches—big ones—like they were twigs.

"Holy cow!" said Ketchum, moving toward the edge.

There was more crackin' and snappin' that set my neck hair to standing up.

"Maybe we should get outa here," I whispered. "Come on, boys."

Me and the boys scrambled down the wooden ladder while Will tried to get the strap unbuckled. We heard a lot of cursing. I guess the grease from the cracklins was making it too slippery to undo. Me and the boys watched the woods, with all the little trees moving around and heard more big snaps and cracks while we piled in the truck. I figured Ketchum was on his own. Probably had his fancy ORV hid close by.

I was having trouble getting the truck to turn over and when I got out to give it a kick (sometimes works) I saw Ketchum teeter kind of on the edge of the platform then go on over. Good thing he still had the safety harness on. It was a hoot seeing him hanging there, like he was trying to fly. He was a wavin' his arms and kicking his legs. I think he yelled at me and I was thinking about going over and trying to lower him, when I see not one, but two big critters coming out of the woods. I jumped back in the truck and asked the Lord to save us. He answered my prayer and the truck give a sputter then started up and we drove off lickety-split. I looked in the one mirror left on the truck and see that Ketchum is still dangling there mad enough to spit nails. He was still trying to get the belt off, and I wasn't sure what was closing in on him, but it looked like two critters like I'd never seen. Not bears or moose neither.

"Wow! Aunt Nettie," said the youngest. "Officer Will is so cool, like Batman flying around on a rope. I want to be a conservation officer when I grow up so I can do fun stuff!"

"I got it all on a video on the phone!" said the oldest. "This will be the most awesome school project in the history of Budworm Middle School!"

I was feeling a little bad about leaving Will dangling but had my two nephews and figure that's a good excuse to skedaddle. I gave a think about going back in a day or two and see if there was anything left of CO Will Ketchum. If he'd gotten out of the fix, I wasn't too worried about him dragging me up in front of Judge Nightshade because my oldest nephew had somehow got a film inside that itty bitty phone that would probably be a tad embarrassing for Ketchum.

* * *

Ketchum had given up flailing around and was struggling to get out his Leatherman to cut himself loose. He heard the racket coming from the woods and figured if it was a bear, he was a sitting duck. He got his knife out and before he could begin sawing at the belt, his cracklin greasy hands let loose the tool, which fell to the ground.

Then not one but two creatures approached. Ketchum closed his eyes and prepared to endure a horrible death. Toivo and Eino Maki, who were second or third cousins twice removed, were wearing their new camo hunting outfits that made them look like a couple of mossy oak walking wookiees.

"Say there Toivo, whatcha think we got here?"

"I think we finally found us Nettie Bramble's hunting stand," Toivo said. "I told yous that if we followed the ATV trail we'd find it. Looks like she's got a good bait pile goin' here, eh?"

"No, I mean what we got danglin' there?" Eino said, pointing at the suspended conservation officer who was twisting slowly in the wind.

"Oh, ain't that Ketchum?" Toivo said. "Whadda doin' there Ketchum? Learning to fly?"

"I think he passed out. He looks kinda limp," said Eino.

"Probably some kind of conservation officer training," Toivo said. "You know, like them Navy Seals that they almost kill to make sure they're up to the job."

"You think we should cut him down?" Eino said.

"Naw, I imagine someone will come looking for him. We don't wanna mess up his training."

The Makis looked up at the unconscious CO who was spinning ever so slowly first clockwise, then counterclockwise.

"So, I guess we leave him danglin', eh?" Eino said.

"Do you smell cracklins?" Toivo said.

"Sure do. Let's go to the Grub Hut and get us something deep fried," Eino said.

They turned toward Ketchum and did a little salute and thanked him for his service.

## Stinkhole Fishing

Ma was watching "her soaps" on her new giant smarty-pants TV and sipping some medicine 'scribed by Dr. Jack Daniels while I was doing something useful, like getting ready to head out on the ice to catch us some fish for supper. I was getting sick of venison. This year's buck was so dry and tough, Ma had to pound the hell out of the meat with a cleated hammer and add half a pound of lard to the fry pan just so's we could choke it down.

"It's them acorns they been gobblin' up," Ma would say when we chewed until our jaws went numb. "Makes 'em tough and gamey. We'd've been better off if yous woulda gone and shot us a cow when that dumbass Lempi Buzzoff wudunt lookin'."

That was just what I needed was to go in front of Judge Nightshade for shooting the neighbor's cow. Anyhow, I was lacing up my mukluks when the cabin door banged open and my two nephews come thundering in. They both ran to our new refrigerator and whipped it open.

"You got any Cokes?" shouted the oldest.

"I wanna orange pop," whined the youngest.

"Quiet you two rug rats!" Ma yelled, "I'm watchin' my soaps. Veronica says she's pregunt and it ain't Chadwick's kid. They's soda pop on the top shelf and some of them double stuffed chocolate cookies inna cupboard. Now shut yer yaps."

"Who isn't Chadwick's kid?" said my Perfect Sister, MarshMarigold, who came in next, followed by her dimwit husband, Tag Alder.

"Veronica's!" Ma said.

"Whose Veronica?" Tag said.

"It's a TV show," M&M snapped. "Now tell them about your latest Most Stupid Idea Ever!"

This got Ma to mute the TV and me to delay my ice fishing, even though I was sweating like a pig in a sauna.

"It's *not* stupid!" Tag said. "It's called repurposing, so it's good for the environment and I'll make a fortune selling them."

"HAH!" said M&M who went to the kitchen to root around.

Me and ma had lived for years in the cabin without 'lectric. Then the Rural 'lectric Company came along and strung some wire down Bramble Road, and after Tag almost burnt the cabin down, we got actual licensed 'lectricians that wired us up proper. Now we could have things like civilized folks, such as a TV and fridge, which I'll admit is pretty good, even if they were gifts from M&M and Tag. Now the two of them think they can march in and take whatever's in the fridge without so much as asking.

"Outhouses!" MarshMarigold sputtered. "We have a yard full of old, stinky plastic outhouses."

"Vault toilets!" Tag spat back. "And they've been completely sanitized."

"What you want with a bunch of privies?" Ma said.

"Ice shanties!" Tag said. "MDOT—you know, the Michigan Department of Transportation—replaced a bunch of their vault toilets with newer models and *gave* these old ones to me for FREE. They're perfect!"

"Yeah, right," M&M said. "Gave them to us so they didn't have to haul them to the dump. Perfectly disgusting."

"Ice shanties?" I asked.

"Yeah!" Tag said. "See, they're perfect to convert to ice shanties and I can sell them for $100 a pop, I betcha."

That perked Ma up a bit. "Say what?"

"Yes, Mother Bramble," Tag said. "See, you take off the toilet seat and the riser and you've got yourself a perfect opening to go over your fishing hole in the ice."

"The only thing's perfect, is the perfect idiot I married," snarled M&M.

"Fishing through a poophole!" I said. "Hot diggity, don't that sound like a good sales pitch. Maybe yous can catch a turd!"

"Ew," M&M said as she munched on a double chocolate cookie. "Hey, boys, bring me another one of these."

My bro-in-law owned Tag's Honey Wagon, and he had a contract with MDOT for pumping out the privies in the rest stops along the highway.

"I bet the guys at the highway garage are laughing their butts off," I said, "getting ya to take a bunch of worn-out crappers off their hands."

Ma cackled a bit and turned off the TV. She took a sip of her medicine. "We called it the stinkhole when we was kids," she said. "Course me and Nettie keep ours out back smellin' sweet as syrup. But when I was a kid—they was 10 of us—it got pretty dang ripe. Plus, I had five brothers that dumped fish guts down 'em. Anyhow, I say it ain't a bad idea."

"Easy for you to say, old woman," I said. "When's the last time you ice fished? I'd give up eating fish before I'd throw my line down some stinkhole in a stupid outhouse."

"Too bad, Nettie," Tag said, "I was gonna give you a free model for demo purposes. I got one in the back of the truck and we could drive it to the lake and slide it out on the ice with the skids I brought. You'd be snug as a slug on drugs."

I knew darn well that there wasn't any such thing as free when it come to my conniving brother-in-law. I figured he was using me to test drive his hair-brained idea.

"What's in it for me?" I said.

"You get a free vault toil—er ice shanty, is what you get. Like I said, I bet they will go for $100 each."

"I wanna cut of the deal before I head out on Misfortunate Lake in that contraption," I said.

"She's right," said my Perfect Sister. "She can have half, because half of nothing is nothing, so you'll owe her nothing."

"Shut yer yap, MarshMarigold," Ma said. "Now I think Tag's got a purty good thing here. Nettie, get yer butt out there and try it out."

"I'll give you ten percent," Tag said.

"Hah!" I said. "Fifty-fifty."

"Sixty-thirty," he countered.

"Seventy-ten," I said. "That's my final offer."

"Deal!"

I wasn't sure what the deal was, but I was ready to pass out from being dressed in six layers of wool, so it was time to move on.

It went okay at first. When we got to Misfortunate Lake, Tag, me, and the boys got the thing out of the truck and slid onto the ice. It was a pukey, faded turquoise color and the roof, which was fake wood shingles, was starting to peel. Inside, there was a good-sized opening where the toilet had been, along with an empty jumbo toilet paper thing on the wall with the cover busted off. Over the toilet hole there was a sign that said:

DO  OT PU    ASH DO  VA T  OIL . Whatever that was s'posed to mean.

"See, the vent is still here," said Tag. "You could have you a little stove to warm up if you wanted. Just put a board over half the opening and you got a platform for the heater. And that tissue holder there still has the spool on it. Yous can put your fishing line on it and attach a handle, and you got a built-in reel! Hand me my ice spud! I'll chop a big hole and you can try 'er out."

Mostly I used a tip-up rod for ice fishing with an upside-down bucket for a stool, then once I pulled in a few, it turned into a fish tote. This was getting a bit fancy for me. Leave it to a guy to take something simple and tangle it all up. Anyways, while Tag was doing all the grunting and chopping, I looked at the busted-up toilet paper holder trying to figure out how to hook up my line.

"There (wheeze wheeze)," Tag said. "You got a hole big enough to pull in a whale!"

I looked into the opening—or stinkhole as Ma called it. "It's kinda big," I said. "It's only supposed to be like maybe six inches, so's a body don't fall in."

Tag leaned over, looking down at it trying to figure out, I guess, how to make it smaller (yous can't) when my two hooligan nephews, who were supposed to stay in the truck, busted into the shanty. Then a couple of things happened. First, there wasn't enough room for everyone, and me and the boys kind of all fell like a cord of wood coming undone and rolled into Tag, who got knocked into the stinkhole head first. Before I could grab his ankle, he slipped away and disappeared. He was right. It was a big hole!

"Boys, out! We gotta get your pa quick!" I shouted.

Except when Wanton tried the door, the lock didn't work and the door was jammed stuck. I start banging on it, thinking about how my Perfect Sister would blame me for her dumb-butt husband drowning under the ice. We all threw our weight against the door, which thinking back was kinda dumb, and she tipped right on over, with the three of us all in a heap.

Then, wouldn't you know, the wind comes up. The direction was perfect for the air to woosh right through the open stinkhole and start pushing us along the ice.

"Yippeee!" shrieked Wiley. He didn't know that we were probably headed out toward the thin spot where Mill Creek comes into Misfortunate Lake. At least one ice fisherman falls through every winter. Sometimes it's spring before they wash up somewheres. I didn't much care for the idea of me and my nephews joining the party at the bottom of the lake.

Well, while we were zippin' along, me and the boys managed to work our way round and, one by one, crawled out the stinkhole. We all sat on the ice and watched the shanty skid along until it hit the thin ice and sure enough, the ugly turquoise box slowly sank mostly out of sight 'til just the top of the vent pipe was showing above the ice shards floating around it.

"Wow!" Wiley said. "We have the coolest time when we're with you Aunt Nettie."

"Yeah!" Wanton piped in. "Majorly awesome. Hey, where's Dad?"

"Daddy!" yelled the youngest. "He fell in the hole."

"Oh crapola!" I said. Not only would these two scallywags be orphans and their mamma a widow, but worse would be them coming to live with me and Ma. Just shoot me and hang me out for the birds to peck clean!

Then we see something coming across the ice, roaring along hell-bent for leather.

"Look!" Wanton said. "A snowmobile. Can I ride?"

"Yeah," whined Wiley. "My feet are froze. I can't walk."

The snowmobile pulled up and skidded alongside us, carrying some good news and some bad news. The good news was that Tag was the passenger. The bad news was that the local conservation officer, Will Ketchum, was driving. Ketchum was all cozy and bundled up in his DNR-issued arctic suit, but Tag was another story. He looked like last year's catch with a bad case of freezer burn.

"This belong to you?" Ketchum said, jerking his head back toward Tag. "Found him crawling out of a hole in the ice."

"Daddy!" shouted Wiley, running over to Tag.

"Chhhhh, chhhhh, chhhhhh," said Tag.

"Dad!" Wanton said. "Can I ride?"

"Caaa, caaaa, caaa," said Tag.

"Well, well, well," said CO Ketchum, sneering at me. "Look who's out fishing. I don't suppose yous have your license on you, do ya Nettie?"

"We weren't fishin', officer," I said. "See, my brother-in-law here was just trying out this new ice shanty, but things kind of went wrong. Right Tag?"

"Wrrrr, wrrrr, wrrrr!" Tag said.

"Ice shanty?" Ketchum said, looking around. "I don't see any ice shanty."

"Uh huh!" Wanton said, pointing to the six inches of vent stack sticking above the water, which was skimming over.

"Oh, I see," said Ketchum. "Now, Nettie, this is much more serious than no fishing license. An ice shanty that goes through the ice has to be pulled out, or yous can get a $500 fine, plus the cost for the DNR to get it out."

"It's Tag's," I said, pointing at my popsicle bro-in-law.

"I want it out today!" Will said. "I gotta get Tag here up to the boat launch. I called for an ambulance. I think he maybe slipped into hypothermia or a coma. Watch the thin ice north of the boat launch. You need to get on shore as far to the south as you can."

I took a gander at Tag and noticed he'd quit blubbering and hadn't blinked for a while. Then the sled roared off and zipped up the boat launch ramp to where an ambulance was parked. When they pulled Tag off the snowmo, his legs stayed like they were still straddling the machine. The ambulance folks couldn't get them to straighten out to put him on the gurney, so they propped him up kind of sitting like on the edge and loaded him up.

"I called his wife and she's on her way to the ER," Ketchum yelled as me and the boys trudged ashore. It wouldn't be the first time M&M had to bail Tag outa the emergency room. Then Ketchum nodded toward the sunk shanty. "I want it out by dark!"

Before I could answer, he climbed into his fancy DNR truck and peeled out like some hotshot race car dude.

"I'm froze!" whined Wiley.

"I'm hungry!" said the other one.

Guess the boys weren't too concerned about their freezer pop.

"Get in the truck," I said. "I bet your pa left the keys in. I got me an idea for getting that thing out."

We were lucky that the current from Mill Creek slowly took the ice shanty toward the boat ramp, breaking through the ice along the north side where it was thin. It got hung up when it hit the launch skid where it rolled over once, and came to rest.

"Perfect!" I said, going round back of Tag's truck where the winch was mounted. After a couple of misses, I finally had a lucky toss and got the winch hook to snag the stinkhole of the shanty and pulled it in real slow.

"Look!" screeched Wiley. "Fishies!"

Darned if the boy wasn't right. When the shanty inched up the boat ramp, a whole slew of real nice whitefish and lake trout come flappin' and floppin' out the stinkhole and onto the cement ramp.

"Let's get 'em boys!" I shouted, grabbing my trusty tote bucket.

Once we headed home, with a nice bucket of fresh fish on the truck floor, Wanton said: "What about the ice toilet? Won't that woods cop get mad?"

"Naw," I said. "That ugly ol' thing'll be gone in a jiffy."

What the boys didn't see was that I'd scrounged up a can of blaze orange spray paint from the truck and wrote on the thing: FREE ICE SHANNY. YOUS HAUL!

# Road Rage Rally: Part I

*Featuring: Bea Righteous, Tami & Evi Maki, and Nettie Bramble*

## Bea Righteous

Well, my heavens, but this was the devil's game for certain. Imagine pitting neighbor against neighbor with some ill-conceived idea that a "little" competition was a wholesome endeavor. Of course, there was a nice first prize, which I could not have cared less about in that the Good Lord has blessed me with uncanny luck on my missionary trips to Sin City and other such decadent destinations, and I find myself quite comfortable. Some might say filthy rich.

However, in spite of substantial and frequent rent hikes at the Gnarly Woods Senior Complex where I reside, said facility is always coming up short for one thing or another and the $5,000 purse would, indeed, be adequate to replace the commercial refrigerator that has been making an ominous gurgling noise and persistently leaking fluids onto the floor of the Gnarly Woods kitchen-of-bad-chicken. In any event, I do feel mandated from higher up to set out on this cockamamie rally. Indeed, I expect that from such a venture the (uh, em) righteous shall emerge victorious and the faithless shall wallow in despair.

Or one would think, unless there was an electric car involved. But as usual, I am getting ahead of the story.

## Tami & Evi Maki

"We could use Big Buck," Tami said to her thrice-removed cousin, Evi. The Maki women were looking at the FaceNook post announcing the "Road Rage Rally" contest to raise money for a beautification project for the Village of Budworm. It wasn't so much the beautification of Budworm that Tami was thinking about, but the $5,000 first prize. Tami and Evi had just opened up The Wikiup Wine and Fudge Shoppe and while business was fair, Tami felt they should add pizza and nachos and other artery-clogging food to the venture, and that would take some capital outlay.

Big Buck was an extensively modified Ford/Chevy/GM truck that belonged to Tami's husband, Toivo. Big Buck had no doors and not much by way of floorboards. Also missing was any remnant of the exhaust system, except the snorkel that allowed for amphibious adventures. Also missing were the interior and exterior mirrors and the front bumper, which had fallen off at around 300,000 miles and had been replaced with a "discarded" utility pole that Toivo had salvaged in the dark of the night.

"I thought the gas tank leaked on that POS truck," Cousin Evi responded. "We could perish in a fiery ball," she added.

"It's fixed with some of that Ape Tape. Hardly leaks a drop now. Same with the oil pan," Tami retorted. "I'm sure not using my car for this rally. I just had it detailed. Besides, Big Buck can go off the beaten path—way off—and that's how we'll win this so-called race."

"You mean cheat?" Evi said.

"Of course not," Tami said. "But one must be creative when interpreting the rules, which we will receive once we pay the $100 Entry Fee."

Evi was only half listening as she was putting out the fudge pieces (several of which she had taste-tested) on the "FREE SAMPLE-TRY ME" wine and fudge tasting table in their shoppe.

"So," Tami said, "I'm going to need your credit card. You can get it back from our winnings."

This was always the way it went. Tami's ideas resulted in another hit on Evi's credit card.

## Nettie Bramble

I figured this would be the perfect solution to our plumbing problem in the cabin; that problem being that we don't have any—plumbing that is. We got 'lectric a while back, but still have a dang hand pump outside, and a privy down the path to the gravel pit.

"So, Ma," I said, "we could win $5,000 in this race, and put a toilet in the cabin."

Ma took a good pull on her medicinal whiskey bottle and crumpled up her already crumpled-up face. "So's you go take a poop right in the cabin?"

"Well, I was thinking we could convert the gun closet into a toilet room," I said. "You flush the thing and it all goes down into the ground."

"I know what a toilet does—sort of. I say using ah outdoor privy gets it where it's agoin' with a lot less a fuss."

"Costs a hundred dollars to get in it," I said.

"That's a lotta liquor," Ma said.

Talking to Ma was a waste of time. I'd need a credit card. Me and Ma didn't have one, so I'd have to get my Perfect Sister, MarshMarigold, to lend me hers. I could give her my saved-up cash from selling mostly legal animal pelts.

## Bea R.

The first rule was that at least two people were required in each vehicle. This meant that I needed to recruit someone—preferably a person with a car we could use, as my Buick was not made for a backwoods adventure.

"Sign me up!" Gnarly resident, Myrtle Gawp, squawked at me, as she adjusted her wig de jour—a jet black bouffant with purple streaks.

"But Myrtle," I said, "you don't have a car, or even a driver's license."

"Figgy said she'd drive," Myrtle said, "and we can use her Tezzlala, whatever the devil that is."

I had hoped that Pastor Goode from my church would partner up with his closest disciple—namely, yours truly—and we could set out on this as a mission to raise funding for one of many needs in the world— or for a new fridge at Gnarly Woods Senior Complex. I was quite taken aback when Pastor Goode proclaimed the road rally to be a form of gambling, and therefore prohibited. Interesting from a clergyman who was more than willing to accept *my* winnings from various short-term investments—namely, slot machines—to put new insulation and air conditioning in the parsonage.

It seemed ordained that I would be saddled with the oversight of Myrtle Gawp—an oversexed senior who could find trouble in a gunny sack. Myrtle and I were crammed into the Gnarly Woods activity director, Linda Figgy's electric car, which was perhaps designed to transport vertically-challenged people from Munchkinland to Oz. Miss Figgy—or Figgy for short—had a penchant of talking to herself, though she claims to have some sort of device attached to her ear called the Blue Fang, apparently to keep in touch with "the mother ship."

Figgy was driving, I was navigating, and Myrtle was just annoying. The first clue was so ridiculously easy that even Myrtle got it—sort of.

"Hot diggidy!" She blurted. "Says here to take time to be holly—"

"I believe that's HOLY not holly, Myrtle," I said.

"Okay, so that makes more sense. Anyways: 'Take time to be holy as you watch for the gold. In the winter he snowshoed, this priest we are told.' Well, it's somethin' Catholic," Myrtle surmised, "since it's talkin' about a priest."

## Tami & Evi

Evi was trying to read a 1983 off-road vehicle map while Tami battled Big Buck's steering wheel that tended to pull severely to the right, then suddenly left. Sometimes it went straight, only to have Tami relax a moment before it resumed its shenanigans and lurched toward a tree, rock, or sheer cliff. They were taking a "shortcut" on a washed-out road that would give a mountain goat a nervous breakdown. Evi felt her stomach churn as she tried to read the map and not look at how close they were to plummeting to their death.

"I still say it's not the highest point in Michigan," Evi said.

"Everyone knows it is," Tami snapped. "There's even a sign pointing the way to the Highest Point in Michigan. The clue said that was where we needed to go."

"Okay," Evi said. "First off, it was a riddle, not a clue. Second, it didn't really tell us that at all, and if it did, why the hell aren't we taking the road that the sign points us to?"

"This is faster, you twit, that's why," Tami snapped. "Read it again."

Tami pulled out a folded-up piece of paper that they were given at the start of the rally. If they made it to the first checkpoint, they'd get the next clue, and so on until the race ended at the final rallying point, where the first to arrive would be declared the winner. Contestants would all be sent to all the same checkpoints, but in a differing order, making the whole thing a fiasco.

"It says, 'In Limbo you know how low you can go, but today as you drive and if you survive you rise for the prize as you climb to the skies.' What a dumb clue."

"It *is* a run-on sentence wrought with prepositional phrases," Tami said.

"It talks about climbing to the sky," Evi said. "Maybe we were supposed to go to the airport and get on a plane, in which case we are soooo going the wrong way."

"Oh no," Tami said. "We are definitely going the right way."

## Nettie B.

So, my Perfect Sister—who's 'bout as sweet as a chaw of root-barb—says I could use her plastic card to sign up for the rally and not even fork over the cash, if I was to let her boys, Wanton and Wiley, come along. She and her lazy-boy hubby, Tag, were fixin' to go on some kind of sewage treatment retreat.

Since the rally rules says you gotta have two or more people and Ma didn't want any part of 'some stupid race to put a crapper in the cabin,' I figured my two pain-in-the-patootie nephews would equal one grown-up, so I was good with that rule. The other rule about having a "licensed" vehicle got me worried, since I don't believe in buying licenses and my truck doesn't even have a back bumper to put one on. Anyhow, Tag said I could go ahead and take the Honey Wagon if I wanted, but he hadn't had a chance to pump her out or fuel up after his last job. Figures.

"Yay! Aunt Nettie," spouted off Wiley when we got underway with our first clue. Wanton was pouting some. I didn't care why, but I suspected it was because he wanted something he couldn't have. He was getting to be one of them tweens who you just as soon feed to the coyotes as look at.

"So, Wanton, read me the dang clue again," I said.

"This is stupid. If I had a *smartphone,* I could get us to the finish line without all these dumb clues and riding around in Dad's stinky truck."

I give him THE LOOK so he knows not to mess with me. "Read the clue, or I'll make you stay with Granny!"

He sighed real loud and uncrumpled a piece of paper. "Says here: 'There's no sweet tooth big enough to fill this order, because it's the world's largest prize way north of the border.'"

"Maybe it's a dentist office!" shouted Wiley. "They fill cavities. Pa had the world's biggest cavity and Dr. Meanie had to like give him all

kinds of stuff to kill the pain so's he could drill but we could still hear him yelling all the way in the waiting room."

This wasn't any dentist. I made a U turn—not easy with the crappy big ol' Honey Wagon—and headed North on US 41.

**(Keep reading and you'll get to part II of the road rally. eventually.)**

## In a Snit

Me and Ma were having us a nice peaceful breakfast of cold pizza and Cokes when the door to the cabin slammed open and about scared us to death.

"What th' ...!" Ma shrieked and jumped up, causing her fake teeth to fall out into her pizza.

My two whirlwind nephews came barging in, arguing about something. They were followed by my Perfect Sister and her idiot husband, who lugged in a carton of beer, or "swamp juice" as Ma calls it, and crammed it into our new fridge. I call my sister "perfect" because she snagged herself a man stupid enough to marry her and then she produced a couple of brats. The fact that I can put food on the table and split a cord of firewood doesn't hold up against it with Ma, who sees getting more bodies in the family as a way to sponge off more people. I call her M&M, even though we all know that her candy coating melted off right before she graduated from high school, if you get my drift.

"We brought you your favorite beer, Mother Bramble," Tag said.

My nephews raced over to me, so I hurried to finish off my pizza before they could grab it.

"Aunt Nettie!" yelled Wanton. "We're gonna stay with you and dig a pit!"

"Are not!" yelled Wiley. "We're gonna build a snare!"

"What are yous doing here?" Ma said, wiping a rubbery glob of cheese off her teeth before she stuffed 'em back in. "That ain't my favorite beer you ninny. You brung the cheap stuff again."

My brother-in-law's cheapness was no secret. One of his "dummy-do-it-yourself" shortcuts almost got the cabin burned down. Ma always said he had in him the stupid *and* cheap traits of the Alder clan. And that was the best you could say of him.

"Can you watch the boys for a while?" MarshMarigold said.

"I was planning to do some fishin'," I said. "I got no time for chasing after those two."

"Yous gotta give us warnin' about bringin' them boys," Ma said.

"Well, Mother, we would if you had a phone," M&M said.

"Got no need," Ma said. "They'd have to string more of them ugly wires," she added.

"You can get a cell phone," Tag said as he popped the top on one of his el cheapo cans of brew and took a gulp.

"I heard cell phones give you cancer of the ear," I said.

"I think it's brain cancer," Tag said.

"That explains why you're such an idiot!" I said.

"Hey!" MarshMarigold said. "Don't call Tag names—at least in front of the boys. Anyhow, I've got to meet up with some of my book club friends and Tag says he's got a Sewer Suckers meeting over in Marquette."

"We get the latest scoop on the poop!" Tag said, yucking it up at his dumb joke.

"What book is yous readin'?" Ma said.

"Um..."

"Humph!" I said. I knew she was meeting up with a bunch of gals and they'd run up their charge cards at some shopping mall and guzzle a lot of la-de-da wine at a fancy restaurant. She never invites me. Says I wouldn't fit in.

"So, how about it?" M&M said.

"Can we stay?" shouted the two brats. "Can we build an animal trap? We got some plans."

"I guess," Ma said and looked at Tag. "But yous owe me some good whiskey—not that rotgut you give me at Christmas."

"Yay!" squealed the two boys.

M&M and Tag left quick before anyone could change their mind.

"I wanna dig a pit and catch some wild animals," Wanton said. "I saw it on TV! They were trying to catch a Bigfoot!"

"No such thing as a Bigfoot," I said.

"Told ya!" said Wiley. "I'm gonna make a snare like a mountain man and catch a panther."

The older one gave his younger brother a smack on the arm. "Is too Bigfoots. There was a whole TV show about it."

"Hey, you hit me. I'm telling!" said the younger one.

"Stop horsing around," I said, "or I'll duct tape yous to chairs and make you sit with granny. Anyhow, even if there was such a critter, some wimpy snare's not gonna do the job."

This got the two boys thinking, which was dangerous.

"We can make a snare hanging over a pit!" said Wiley.

"Yeah," said Wanton. "Then we're sure to catch him."

"We got a snare and a pit. Cool!" Wiley said. "It's a snare-pit," he added.

"Hey, we can call it a SNIT for short!" Wanton said.

"Way cool! We'll build a SNIT," Wiley said.

The only snit I had ever seen was the mood Ma got in when she was running short of her 'scription from Dr. Jack Daniels. But I figured digging a big hole would keep the two scallywags busy for a while. In fact, there was a pretty good hole already started that Tag had made when he dug up some dirt to fill in the old outhouse pit. If I put the boys down there, maybe they'd dig up some worms to boot and once they were tuckered, we'd go fishin'.

So we dragged a couple shovels and a big rope outa the shed and the boys started working on their SNIT.

"Now make her a little deeper you two," I said, "and wider at the bottom so's yer critters can't get out." I figured that would keep them going for a while. I was pleased that the boys got down a good five feet before they hit clay and pooped out. And they collected a fair batch of fat crawlers besides.

"Hey, where do we hang the snare?" Wiley said as we dragged him out of the hole. He spit out some dirt and rubbed his mouth. Then he started to get all crybaby. "I wanna catch a panther with the snare!"

"Yeah. There's no tree around. You gotta have a snare hooked to a tree limb that's bent down and pops up and catches the Bigfoot," Wanton said.

Now Wiley was blubbering. "Panther! It's for a panther."

"Quit snivelin' or I'll make you brats go back to the cabin," I said. "We just gotta make something to hang the noose from and you'll have your SNIT."

About twenty minutes later we had a tripod made out of canoe paddles and a big limb balanced over the pit. We used the rope to lash things together and left some slack and made up a noose. We were about as likely to catch a Bigfoot, or anything for that matter, as we were to have one of them flying saucers land in the weeds out back. But the boys were pleased until the older one piped up.

"We need to have bait. What do Bigfoots eat?" he said.

"Panthers eat raw meat," Wiley said. "Can we have some raw meat, Aunt Nettie?"

I was thinking about looking for something dead out on the highway, but it was getting hot and things get pretty ripe on a hot day. Then I remembered the leftover pizza. Ma had dozed off before she finished hers.

"Wiley, run and get the pizza off Granny's plate. Everything likes pizza, so we'll use that."

"Yay!" the boys yelled.

* * *

"You think we caught anything in the SNIT yet?" asked one of the boys while we were loafing at the crick. We'd caught a nice mess of fish that Ma could fry.

"Do you think the pizza is still there or maybe a bear or something stole it," Wiley asked.

"Dunno," I said. "When we gut the fish, we can throw the innards in the SNIT. That might do it." Babysitting was beginning to wear on me. "It's gettin' late. We should head on back," I said. "When's your ma and pa picking you up?"

"Tomorrow, I guess," said the older.

Dang. The Alders had tricked me and Ma. Again.

We gathered up our stuff and headed back to the cabin. The boys rushed up to the SNIT and looked in.

"There's something in here!" shouted Wanton. "A baby Bigfoot!"

"No! We caught a panther," shouted Wiley.

Turns out it wasn't any baby Bigfoot or panther, but a chubby 'ol porcupine down there, munching away on a slab of pizza. It looked up, its beady eyes staring at us. The snare was still dangling over the pit, but the pizza bait had been picked clean. I couldn't figure for the life of me how a porcupine got the bait off that noose. There's nothing slower or clumsier than a porky; that's why they're flattened all over the highway. Then I see a second set of eyes.

"Hey! It's a raccoon," Wanton said, pointing into the SNIT.

Well, that explained it. Raccoons could get anywhere. I was surprised, though, how a raccoon and porcupine seemed all chummy down there, sharing Ma's leftover pizza.

"We gotta get them out!" Wiley said. "If a panther falls in, he'll eat them!" Then he started blubbering again. I swear, that kid's got more waterworks than a busted dam.

"Okay, okay, don't get all worked up," I said. "Go on and fetch a big limb."

"What for?" Wanton said.

"Just git!" I said.

The boys scurried off and soon come back dragging a good-sized limb. We stuck the thing in the hole and skedaddled.

"Them critters should be out by morning," I said, dusting off my hands. "Let's go get granny out of her stupor and have some fresh fish."

"Yay!" cried the two boys as they ran into the cabin and slammed the door open. I figured that would wake the old woman and maybe sober her up.

We were all settled in for the night, watching Wheel of Fortune on the TV when we heard a commotion outside.

"Whaaaa" Ma said, waking up from her snooze.

"Sumthin' out there," I said.

"Bigfoot!" hollered Wanton.

"Panther!" hollered Wiley.

"Probably jist a bear," Ma said. "Nettie, get the shotgun and run it off."

"You run it off, old woman!" I said. "I told you we shoulda got a dog. This here's a perfect time to have a dog."

Ma waved me off and pointed at the double-locked closet where we stashed the shotgun.

So, I got my gun and a flashlight to go see what in heck all the ruckus was about. I heard a lot of noise, sounding angry, coming from the SNIT, like something was not real pleased to be in there. And there was an awful bad smell—a skunk for sure. Next thing I saw was a truck hid in the woods. Best of my recollection, Bigfoots and panthers don't drive trucks. We'd caught us a trespasser. Probably out to steal some of the valuable stuff we keep around in the weeds.

The cabin door banged open and the two boys come barreling out.

"Git back here you two!" Ma shouted from the door, but they still came full speed, then skidded to a halt at the edge of the pit.

The three of us tiptoed over to the SNIT. The tripod that was holding the snare was tipped over. We crept up and I shined the flashlight down the hole. Several sets of eyes glared up except the pair of eyes looking at me over the top of the pit.

"What stinks?" the boys said, holding their noses.

"BRAMBLE! Get me the (bleep) outa here!" said a voice from the pit.

I shined my flashlight over to the part-hid truck and seen the DNR seal on the door.

"Who's there?" I said.

"It's a talking Bigfoot!" said Wanton. "It stinks like one anyway."

"It said a bad word," said Wiley.

"It's me, you stupid twit, get me the (bleep) outa here or I'll put you in chains and drag you before Judge Nightshade!"

"Ketchum? What are you doing in the SNIT?" I said.

"You'd be in a SNIT too," he said, "if you were sharing a (bleeping) pit with all these (bleeping) varmints."

"Climb out for crying out loud. It's not that deep," I said.

"Oh, gee, why didn't I think of that? You elbow! I tried that and the (bleeping) bank keeps crumbling away and I'm stuck down here with a (bleeping) zoo. What is this—some kind of illegal animal trap? Look Bramble, I've been quilled, skunked, and bit. I'll have to get rabies shots. Get me out NOW or I swear... Ow! (Bleep, bleep, bleep)."

"He said a lot of bad words," Wiley said. "Boy, it sure does stink!"

"Hey, isn't that the cop that keeps getting mad at you Aunt Nettie?" Wanton said.

Yep. We had trapped Conservation Officer Will Ketchum. Since I was pretty sure he would chain me up and drag me into court, me and the boys found the snare rope and tossed it to Ketchum. Thing was, we weren't strong enough to pull him out, so I went to his truck and the keys were in the ignition. I started 'er up and backed up to the pit. We got the rope hooked to the bumper and Ketchum managed to pull himself up. He was a-gruntin' and wheezin' pretty bad. Worse thing though was that the smell got worse.

"You are in so much trouble!" he snarled, poking a finger in my face.

"Now wait a darn minute, Ketchum, what in heck were yous doing snooping around my place after dark?" I said, pointing right back at him. "Way I look at it, you're trespassing."

"Hah! I got a reliable source said you were fishing down at the crick. I was looking for evidence—and there's a fresh load of fish guts down there in that (bleeping) pit stinking to high heaven. That is, unless you got a license for all the fish that belonged to those guts?" he said, trying to pull a quill out of his arm. "Ow! (bleep)."

"So, you come during Wheel of Fortune in the dark to check my fishin' license? Who the heck is this *reliable source*?"

"We ate them for supper!" Wiley said. "A whole mess."

"Shut up," Wanton said, poking his brother.

"Ow (bleep)," Wiley said.

"Watch your language," I said. "That's a grownup word."

"Well, ANYWAY," Ketchum said, "you got an illegal animal trap out there. That's a jail-time offense."

"We were gonna get a Bigfoot!" Wanton said.

"No! A panther," Wiley said. "Besides, it's not an animal trap, it's a SNIT."

"I don't care what you call it, it's illegal," Ketchum said.

"Now just keep your blasted bloomers on," I said. "It isn't actually a trap."

"That so?" Ketchum said.

I pulled him aside, then catching a strong whiff of skunk, did some distancing. "I told the boys that's we were digging. But it's really a new hole for the privy." I pointed to the nearby outhouse. It was a quick think on my part. We didn't need a new hole because me and Ma had

Tag dig a new one just a couple of weeks before, but I wasn't a Bramble if I couldn't be quick on my feet.

"Well (bleep)," he said.

"What's goin' on out there?" Ma shouted from the cabin. "I smell a dang skunk!"

"Yup," I answered, "yous sure do. "But he's leaving."

Ketchum gave me an ugly look then said, "Later."

The two boys were jumping all over the place, wound up like an eight-day clock. "This was the best most awesome time ever, Aunt Nettie!" they shouted.

I watched Ketchum limp over to his truck and pull himself up. I could see a porky quill stickin' out of the seat of his pants. He slid in and let out a yelp that got the coyotes in the next county howling.

"You bet yer patootie," I said. "Best time ever."

# Twisted-Tree Hideout

"Why in heck don't you jist git a license?"
Ma said.

I was cleaning up my hunting
shotgun complaining to Ma about
how Ketchum had jinxed my tree
stand from the previous year. Deer
season was just round the corner, and
the bum was watching me like I was
some kind of backwoods terrorist.

"Because," I said, "it's not right,
that's why. Plus, a combo hunting/fishing license
costs more than a case of that rotgut you drink."

"It ain't rotgut," Ma said. "This's good stuff Tag give me fer my
birthday."

I snorted because there was no purpose in arguing with Ma. To her,
anyone who supplies her with booze is up for sainthood. 'Course, I do
everything else for us, like lug in water from the pump, pay all the bills
(turns out that 'lectricity and satellite TV cost money), put food on the
table, get her *real* medicine at the drugstore, and shovel a path to the
privy all winter. My bro-in-law, Tag, gets on Ma's good side by
keeping her soused. Also, he and MarshMarigold produced two hellion
boys that keep popping in without an invite.

"So no deer meat 'cause of Will Ketchum, eh?" Ma said. "And him
kin and all. Ain't right."

"Ketchum would send his granny to jail for a violation," I said.
"And he's watching me like a vulture. But he's wasting his time
because I got an idea."

Just then the door banged open and those two nephews I mentioned
came tearing into the cabin, followed by Tag and MarshMarigold. It

was a good thing my shotgun wasn't loaded or I'd of probably taken out half the family.

"Holy moly," squeaked Ma. "Don't yous ever knock?"

"Hello Mother Bramble," Tag the suck-up said, giving Ma a peck on the cheek. "How's my favorite mother-in-law today?"

Barf. Like he'd have two mother-in-laws. Ma gets all goofy and flashes Tag a smile, which is minus a few teeth and a little lopsided because her botched harelip surgery.

"We brought you something, Mom," said MarshMarigold.

"Yeah, we can see them two brats you brung," Ma said.

When Tag and MarshMarigold want to pawn their boys off to us, they usually bring some kinda bribe. Maybe booze for Ma, or fancy soap or shampoo for me, which I got no use for.

"We got you some apples!" yelled Wanton.

"We took the boys to the Crestview Apple Orchard for some quality family time," M&M said.

"I told them to get lots of nice shiny apples for Grandma Bramble and Aunt Nettie," Tag said.

"You said to give them the ones with worms!" Wiley piped up.

"Figures," I muttered.

"We were just kidding!" said Tag with a fake chuckle.

"Anyway, there's a couple bushels sitting on the porch. And we were hoping you could watch the boys this afternoon so we can make a trip into Marquette to do some shopping," MarshMarigold said.

"Why can't you take them?" I said. "They're big enough to walk around a store."

"Well, we wanted to, you know, do some early Christmas shopping," MarshMarigold said, winking like she had a tick crawling in her eyeball.

Yay!" yelled the boys.

"Hah!" I said. "It's not even November."

"We like to start early," M&M said.

"So, we'll be back after supper," Tag said as he and my Perfect Sister split faster'n a whitetail in the gun sights.

Turns out that the apples were mealy and wormy and no good for anything except deer bait, which was fine with me. Question was, how to get a bait pile going without CO Ketchum sniffin' it out. No way I could hide anything from that pain-in-the-butt, so I'd came up with the idea that I'd need to hide them in plain sight, and maybe my two nephews could be part of my cover.

"So boys," I said. "Help me load up the apples in the truck. We're going to the orchard."

"But we just came from the orchard," Wanton said.

"I don't wanna pick any more apples!" Wiley said. "I got a sore thumb from picking and I think I ate a worm when I bit into one. I hate apples! Waaaaa."

"Shut up!" Wanton snapped.

"Quiet!" I snarled. "Yous'll wake Granny, and I might just make you stay here with her. The orchard we're going to isn't for picking."

The boys had figured a while back that it was better to hang out with their Aunt Nettie than fetch and carry for Granny and be forced to watch her soaps and game shows.

The orchard we headed for was pretty much played out, and the trees had grown all wild and gnarly. Was that way even back when I was a kid and hid out there trying to get away from my mean sister. Other stuff had sprung up in the orchard, like pine and popple trees. I had me a spot picked out that I figured Will Ketchum would never suspect as a deer blind. It was a good hiding spot because it was three trees—apple, pine, and popple—that had twisted around like a corkscrew as if a tornado had grabbed and braided them and left a nice pocket in the middle. When I was a kid, I called it the twisted-tree hideout. I could fit in there and sit on a root that was shaped like a seat. I mighta been smaller then.

Still, there was room to sit in there and wait for a big buck to come by. Except none ever did, because the apple tree that was twisted up with the pine and the popple hadn't put out apples for a long time, so no deer. Also, I never tried to fit a shotgun in with me. I figured that some modifications were needed to make it work. And I also needed to be sure that Ketchum was somewhere else. That's why I set up a "decoy" tree stand in Gnarly Woods, about as far from the apple orchard as you could get. I went to the fake hunting stand regular to pretend I was getting ready for the hunt. I knew Ketchum was watching, sharpening his pencil so's he could write me a ticket for no license and drag me into court to face crabby ol' Judge Nightshade.

"Here we are boys," I said as we pulled up to the twisted-tree hideout.

"Wow!" they shouted. "Way cool!"

"This's a secret," I told them. "It's Aunt Nettie's hideout. I hid from your ma when we were kids."

The two boys crawled into the opening that worked for a door.

"Alright you two, get outa my way so's I can check it out," I said.

The boys came out and started climbing the trees. I got inside and sat on the root seat. It poked me in the butt, so I figured I'd need to get some kinda cushion. And I couldn't see a thing. If a deer was to stroll by, I'd never spot it through the gaps in the twisted trees, let alone be able to get a shot off. I'd need a saw to cut some decent size holes—kind of like the little windows soldiers looked through back when they holed up in forts. Ma and I visited the one there by the Mackinac Bridge. Of course it was fake. And everywhere you went, they were selling fudge and tee shirts.

Anyhow, I figured if I put a few apples around the twisted tree, deer might come round and by hunting season, I'd have my pick of six, eight, and maybe even ten pointers.

Except it occurred to me that I had a problem. When you're dealing with the likes of Will Ketchum, you gotta think like him. If Ketchum spots the twisted trees, I can tell him that me and the boys were just building them a hideout to play in. But having apples strewn around under a tree that don't give apples might cause him to start thinking something's fishy.

I looked up in the trees where my nephews were climbing like a couple of monkeys. Those two were as spoiled as half the apples in the bushel baskets we'd dragged over. Their ma and pa were already getting them a bunch of fancy stuff for Christmas. When I was a kid, we were poor and Ma just knitted me and MarshMarigold a bunch of stupid hats and mittens. They had more holes than a slab of Swiss cheese from where Ma dropped stitches. The more eggnog she drunk, the more stitches she dropped.

Thinking about Christmas got me an idea. I remembered the plastic apples we'd got from the thrift store and hung from the branches of our Christmas tree, along with popcorn and pinecones. That was before we had 'lectricty and now we can string some lights.

"Boys!" I shouted, "We're gonna do some Christmas decorating."

"Yay!" the two shouted as they scrambled down the twisted trees.

We drove back to the cabin and I made the boys stay in the truck while I grabbed a saw from the shed and went into my bedroom to dig out the plastic apples from the Christmas junk stored under my bed. Ma was snoring in front of the TV while some commercial was on for a button you push to get help. I figure if Ma falls, she can just sleep it off wherever she lands.

Back at the twisted tree hideout, I sent the boys up to hang the plastic apples on the branches. I worked on making my shootin' holes bigger and strapped a life jacket on the root seat for a cushion. The boys scrambled down just as I was scattering around some real apples, looking like they'd just fallen off the tree. I put the extra apples back in the truck and just as I looked up at the job the boys had done, I heard a car engine.

"It's that cop that doesn't like you, Aunt Nettie!" shouted Wanton.

"Wow!" said Wiley, always impressed by the DNR's snappy uniform.

CO Ketchum strutted up to us, looking all crisp and smug. "What's going on here, Bramble?" he said.

"What's it look like?" I snarled, buying a little time.

"We're building a hideout. But don't tell anyone because it's a secret!" said blabbermouth Wiley.

"That so?" Ketchum said.

"Yup," I said. "Keeping my nephews busy so's they stay outa trouble. Hee hee."

Ketchum walked around the tree and looked down at the apples. Then he looked up. "Huh. Will you look at that? This ol' tree is putting out some fruit. Might be a good hunting spot." He gave me a smirky look. "I might have thought that these apples on the ground were put there by someone, but then I see there's some up there in the branches."

"My brother and I put them—ow!" Wiley said, as his brother punched him.

"Shut up you dope!" Wanton said.

"Waaaaaa!"

"Quiet both of yous or no ice cream later!" I said. I hadn't planned on ice cream but needed something to shut them up.

Ketchum tended to ignore my nephews, which was good. Then he looked up again. "Some nice places to set up a tree stand," he said. Guess it didn't occur to him that there was an even better place for a deer blind *inside* the trees. Ketchum's not as smart as he thinks.

I looked up. "Don't know about that." That's when I noticed something that I hoped to heck Ketchum didn't notice. The boys had attached the plastic apples to all three twisted trees and any fool knows that pine and popple trees don't grow apples.

"Of course, how many tree stands does a person need?" he said, giving me a smirky look. "I spotted a nice one there at the edge of Gnarly Woods, not too far from the old folks' home. Can't image any of those senior citizens wanting to climb up in a tree stand."

This time I just shrugged and hoped he thought the sweat that was starting to run down my forehead was because of the decoy tree stand in Gnarly Woods and not something I spotted up in the twisted trees.

After me and the boys had some Moose Tracks ice cream, we headed back to the cabin where Ma was cooking supper.

"Where you been at?" Ma snapped, as she poked at something frying in the skillet. "Them boys must be starved. I fried us some scrapple. Sit!"

I didn't see a problem with having ice cream before supper, especially since Ma's scrapple could be made from about anything, including parts of a critter best fed to the dog, if we had a dog. I was jittery, wanting to get back to the twisted-tree hideout/deer blind before Ketchum caught on. Since the two nephews were bottomless pits, they plunked down at the table and was ready to chow down on Ma's scrapple that they doused in ketchup.

"Not hungry," I said as I headed to the door.

"You want me to save you back some?" Ma said.

"You can feed mine to the dog!" I said.

"Ain't gotta dog," Ma said. "Where you goin'? It's gonna storm any minute."

"You're full of *scrapple,* old woman. Not a cloud in the sky," I said.

"She's comin'," Ma said. "My hip is tunin' up pretty good."

Ma and her arthritis. Trouble was, she was most often right. It was almost dark when I reached the twisted-tree hideout, and I saw lightning flashing across the sky. I also seen some other light flicking around the orchard that wasn't lightning. I knew right off what it was—that dang bright light that COs have on their trucks to flush out poachers. I was certain as a storm was brewing that Ketchum was shining his spotlight up the twisted trees, looking at something. So I pulled off into the weeds and killed my one headlight and watched to see what Ketchum was up to.

A flash of lightning lit things up for a second and I saw Ketchum's truck inching toward the twisted tree. A clap of thunder wasn't far behind. Ma's storm was coming. Ketchum kept his spotlight on the twisted trees and got outa his truck. He kept looking up, like a hound after a squirrel. Then he commenced trying to climb the trees, which isn't easy for a fella that's carrying a lot of gadgets on a belt around his middle, not to mention the extra weight he's put on from too many pasties and fish fries.

But darned if he didn't make it up into the trees where he reached for one of them plastic apples. I'm thinking he noticed first off that the apple's not real because he tried to take a bite. Then maybe he noticed that he picked it from a white pine tree, which is part of the twisted-tree tangle, and even if the apple was real, white pines give cones, not apples.

"Bramble!" he yelled out into the orchard. "You are in deep doodoo!"

I scrunched down in my seat, wondering if he somehow knew I was close by. I swear Ketchum's got some kind of Northwoods voodoo going for him.

But I had the Lord on my side, because just as Ketchum started to shinny down the trees, a humongous bolt of lightning zigzagged from the sky and hit the twisted-tree hideout, snapping off the limb he was glommed onto. Ketchum and the limb hit pretty hard and I sat in my truck wondering if I should go help or skedaddle. Then I saw that the twisted trees had some smoke coming from them and a couple of seconds later the whole clump burst into flames. That got ol' Ketchum moving, and me too! I'd just as soon face Ma's scrapple than explain to a ticked off CO about plastic apples growing from a white pine tree.

I found out later on, Ketchum couldn't get his hair to quit stickin' straight up and was giving everybody static shocks. I also heard he claimed he got hurt trying to rescue an orphan bear cub from a burning tree, or some cockamamie story. Guess he didn't want to admit that he'd climbed a rotten tree in a thunderstorm to pick plastic apples.

* * *

Turns out the twisted-tree hideout got burnt to the ground. That wasn't a big deal though, since I had my "decoy" tree stand over in Gnarly Woods. I could hunt free and easy there since CO Ketchum was out on medical leave all through huntin' season with a busted collar bone, cracked ribs, sprained ankle, and some kind of mental breakdown. Me and the boys took him over some apple butter we'd made from all them wormy apples Tag and MarshMarigold gave us. Will's wife—she's a real nice gal—said she see to it he ate it every morning on his toast.

# Turkey and the Law

Ma was tuned into one of her "soaps," which to me was nothing but a bunch of dummies who didn't seem to know where babies come from. First off, Linda is doing the hoochie coochie with her boss, Hank, who far as I could tell is older'n dirt and probably had to take one of them little blue pills, if you get my drift. He's in a pickle because he knows his wife, Martha, will take him to the cleaners in divorce court. Especially since she has some kind of ailment so's she can't walk and needs full-time care. Probably why ol' Hank had the wandering whatnots. And Ma was acting like these were real people and took it way too serious.

I wasn't wasting time with worrying about some stupid TV show because turkey season had just opened and I was busy getting my shotgun and "magic gobbler" turkey caller ready to hunt a big tom. I've said it before, I don't believe in buying a huntin' license, especially turkey, since you got to pay just to get in a drawing to *maybe* buy a license. Bunch of hooey, but I'm religious about huntin' in season, at least usually.

"You rotten sumbitch!" Ma shrieked. "Yer wife's inna wheelchair, and that hussy yous hooked up with ain't nothin' but a…"

It was hard to tune Ma out, with all the shouting.

I was testing the sights on my shotgun when a couple of cannonballs, Wanton and Wiley, came blasting into the cabin causing Ma to jump outta her chair. Good thing my gun wasn't loaded or I might'a shot a hole in the ceiling. Close behind were the Bickersons arguing something about what color to paint their fancy indoor toilet.

"Pink is a sissy color," Tag said.

"It's not pink," MarshMarigold snapped back. "It's *tropical fusion!*"

"Sounds girly to me. I want brown."

"Poop brown! You men. All your taste is in your mouth," M&M said.

"Hey, Mother Bramble," Tag said, going over to Ma and kissing the air in front of her face. "You enjoying the television? What's on?"

"I guess," Ma said. "Marsh is right, you mens'r a sorry bunch of buttcheeks."

"Huh?" Tag said, looking at the TV. He shrugged and went over to the fridge and began rummaging around.

"Brownies'r in the cupboard," Ma said. "Ain't no beer left if that's what yer lookin' for."

"Just a Coke," Tag said. "Got to drive to Home Depot and pick up some girly paint for the bathroom."

"And towels, a new shower curtain, and rugs," MarshMarigold added. "And one of those shelf things that go over the toilet."

"Which I'll have to assemble," Tag said popping the top on a Coke. "So, Mother Bramble, the boys are hoping to hang out with their granny and Aunt Nettie instead of being bored—"

"More like you want to be shed of them for your la-de-da shopping," I said. "They can't come with me. I'm going turkey huntin'."

"Yaaaaaay! I want to shoot a turkey. BLAM! BLAM! BLAM!" Wanton yelled, pretending to hold a gun that he waved around the room.

"Waaaaaa," squalled Wiley. "That's mean, to kill things. Wanton stomped on a spider for no reason and killed it. And he—"

"Shut up you two!" Ma shouted. "Martha's about to wheel in on her two-timin' husband and the floozie. Ooooo, wish she had a gun. Then we'd see us some real action."

Everyone shut up.

"Dang, we have to wait 'til tomarra," Ma said. "I hate when they do them cliphangings."

"Cliffhangers," my perfect know-it-all sister said. "Anyway, we're fine with the boys going hunting with you, Nettie. Tag showed them all about gun safety."

"I did?" Tag said as he stuffed a brownie in his mouth. The two boys in question were also wolfing down brownies.

"Sure," MarshMarigold said as she edged toward the door. "Come on sweetums," she cooed. "Time's a-wasting."

And with that the two scampered out the door like a couple of weasels outa the henhouse.

I eyed my nephews thinking it would probably be child cruelty leaving them with their granny, who had already put her medicinal booze in her coffee cup. She'd be out like a light in a few minutes, and probably wouldn't notice if the two brats set the cabin on fire.

Wanton grabbed my Magic Gobbler and gave it a good blow. Except he was blowing in the wrong end, so it just made a whooshing noise.

"I wanna try!" whined Wiley, trying to reach my turkey caller that his brother was holding above his head. "I wanna blow in it," he sniveled, jumping and grabbing at air.

I walked over to the oldest and snatched my Magic Gobbler. "Now listen up you two, if you're going huntin' with me, there's gonna be some rules, or I'll leave you right here with granny."

"Like hell!" Ma said. "My game show 'Deal or Doom' is comin' on. Tag says he signed me up so's I can win what them players win. I gotta be watchin' and I don't need no rug rats around makin' trouble."

Of course I knew Ma would be snoring away by the end of the show and not know which end was up when she came to.

There'd been turkeys everywhere all winter, looking for handouts, and now that spring was here, they were as scarce as gills on a donkey. But I had done some scouting around and found their range to be around the Gnarly Woods/dead apple orchard. It was good turkey territory, with woods and open area. I'd seen a nice tom struttin' around a week or so ago, showing off to the gal turkeys. He'd stuff and roast up real nice once I got him. I'd set up a turkey blind just in the woods where I could get a clear shot once ol' Tommy goes parading around.

Me and the boys piled into the truck and headed to the orchard. I warned the boys that if they were too noisy, I'd leave them in the truck. Wiley had figured out how to blow my Magic Gobbler and was doing a pretty good job of it, even if it was driving me crazy. I figured if the boys switched off using my turkey caller, they'd be occupied, and I'd have my hands free for a good shot.

We parked at the end of a two-track and set off walking, keeping real quiet. I had on my mossy oak camo outfit and the boys had their camo jackets me and Ma got them for Christmas. They were all jazzed up but trying to be quiet. It about scared us all out of our drawers when we flushed out a flock of turkeys. They flapped and gobbled all running into each other then took wing leaving a cloud of feathers floating in the air.

"Wow, Aunt Nettie!" Wanton said. "How come you didn't shoot?"

"I don't try to shoot when they're on the wing," I said as I watched the flock settle about 100 feet away, not too far from my blind. Truth was, I'd been happy to take a shot, except I didn't have a chance to pull my shotgun up to my shoulder before they were out of range. Plus, wing shots were a waste of ammo.

"Hey!" said the youngest. "Look at these giant eggs."

Wiley was squatted down and looking at a nest made of sticks, leaves, and twigs that held a jumble of turkey eggs. "Can I have one? Can I?" he said, jumping up and down.

I looked off at the flock of turkeys, now headed back our way, likely not happy with us messing around their eggs. Turkeys are dumb and big and can get real mean when you mess with their eggs.

"If he gets one, I get one too!" said the oldest. "This would be great for extra credit for school! I could hatch it and everything and maybe get an A in science. We're studying reproduction."

I saw there were a good number of eggs in the nest and didn't see any reason the boys couldn't each have one, especially in the name of science.

"Okay, but just one each and put them someplace warm, but make sure you don't sit on 'em," I said.

The boys each carefully picked up an egg and slipped them into one of their sixteen pockets that come standard with camo jackets.

"Okay, so we'll just go ahead and be real quiet so's that we don't scare off the turkeys before we get to my blind." I took my Magic Gobbler back from Wiley and slid it into my pocket.

"I'm gonna name mine Tom!" Wiley said.

"Shhhhh," I hushed. "Real quiet."

"That's dumb," Wanton said. "What if it's a girl turkey?"

"I said shush."

We were all quiet and practically tiptoed along the trail when something bright flashed off in the woods. Could'a been the sun shining off a puddle of water or maybe some trash. But no such luck.

"Oh, shoot," I hissed. "Don't move!" I said to the boys who froze in their tracks.

We slipped into the edge of the woods, and I crept into a cove to investigate the glint of light. "You got to be kidding," I said under my breath. The glint was from a truck that belonged to the DNR, and the words Conservation Officer was plain as day in the door decal. Probably the sun was reflecting off the outside mirror.

"Well, well, well," came a voice as a shape appeared out of the morning mist and stepped into a clearing by the truck.

"Ketchum!" I said.

"Bramble," he said.

"Wow! It's the woods cop!" shouted Wiley.

"Can we see your gun?" said Wanton.

Will Ketchum, who was nothin' but a nasty thorn in my side, nodded at the boys and give me a snug look. "Nice day for a walk in the woods, eh Bramble?" he said.

"We're gonna hunt turk—" started the youngest, until his brother gave him a good jab in the ribs.

"Hunt what?" Ketchum said. "I see a nice blind over there. Perfect for turkey hunting."

"We're just having a nice nature walk, huntin' for, ah, turkey eggs," I blubbered without thinking.

"Oh, now Nettie," Ketchum said. "There's no law against hunting turkeys. That is, so long as you have a license and of course permission to hunt here, since this is private land. There is a law against disturbing turkey nests and taking eggs."

"But there were lots—ow!" blurted the youngest, getting another jab in the ribs.

"See, I tol' the boys we'd look for some dinosaur eggs. You know, kind of like a snipe hunt." I give Ketchum a couple of winks pretending I was having some fun with the boys.

"Something wrong with your eye, Bramble?" Ketchum said.

"Dinosaur eggs. Way cool!" Wanton said, playing along. "For a school project," he added.

That's my boy!

"That so?" Ketchum said. "And you need the gun because...?" he said, pointing at my shotgun.

"Well, hee hee," I said. "Never know when a real dinosaur is gonna pop up." I give him another big wink and nodded toward my nephews.

"Yeah said Wiley. "Arrrrgggggrrr," he added, clawing at the air.

"Did you know that birds evolved from dinosaurs?" Wanton said.

"Nope, I didn't," Ketchum said. "I don't suppose you have a turkey hunting license on you, Bramble. You know, just in case you were to mistake one for a dinosaur," he said, nodding toward the flock of turkeys eyeing us from about 75 feet away.

"No sir," I said. I can't get a license this year because I didn't get in the drawing in time."

"Uh huh. What a shame. And that blind over there," he said, jerking his head toward the edge of the woods. "That yours?"

"Well, could be," I said. "But it's just a place to sit and, ah, birdwatch."

"Really? Spotted anything rare?"

"Nope," I said.

He looked at me real hard and snickered. "Well, Nettie, boys, have a good *dinosaur* hunt.

With that, he tipped his hat and gave me another tough-guy look. "Got my eye on you, Bramble."

Then he melted into the woods.

* * *

Me and the boys decided to head back to the cabin, since I wasn't likely to get a turkey that day. We got there and saw that Tag and MarshMarigold beat us home and they were at each other like a couple of roosters sharing one hen. Ma was sound asleep with the TV going but on mute.

"I told you we should have called first," M&M said.

"Hey, it's your thing. I'm just the hired help."

"Mom, Dad!" shouted Wiley. "We have some dinosaur eggs. I'm gonna hatch mine and keep it as a pet."

"That's nice, sweetie pie," M&M said. "I'm going to have to accessorize by ordering online now and try to match the paint."

"Whatever," Tag said, opening the fridge. I expect he frowned because he remembered there wasn't any beer.

"It's a turkey egg, you dummy," Wanton said. "I can get extra credit at school if it hatches."

Tag and Marsh stopped in their tracks and look at their boys. "Don't call your brother a dummy," Marsh said. "Hatch what?" She looked at me.

"Turkeys," I said.

"We have to get a nest box and the heating pad and stuff," Wanton said. "I can take pictures on my phone. I'll show them to Mr. Werme, my teacher, and do a presentation and everything. It will be awesome."

"Hmmm," Tag said. "Aha! I thought you said you were out of beer."

Ma was known to hide her hooch behind sour milk and moldy food containers to throw Tag off the trail. The Alder clan finally left about the time Ma woke up and staggered off to the outhouse.

We didn't give any more thought about turkey eggs until one day the Alder clan busted into the cabin and Wanton showed me a pitcher on his phone.

"Look, Aunt Nettie, Granny, they hatched! Dad was there when they did and he's feeding them when we're in school. Mr. Werme said I will get all kinds of extra credit. He told me I should learn about something—printing? I can't remember."

Then we had quite a show when Tag shuffled in with two little fuzzballs running along behind, peeping up a storm. "Imprinting," muttered Tag as he went to the kitchen and opened the fridge. "They think I'm their ma."

"It's the law of nature," MarshMarigold said while she watched her boys take a video of their pa and his brood. "You know, birds of a feather…"

"Always said you got you a turkey," Ma said, then burst out cackling.

We all had a good laugh at that. All of us except Tag, that is.

# Road Rage Rally: Part II

### *And so, the race continues...*

### Team Bea Righteous

"We need to find a place to plug in," Linda Figgy said. She pointed at the tiny dashboard of the electric Tezzlala car that she, Myrtle Gawp, and I were crammed into. There was an ominous red blinking idiot light, which under ordinary circumstances would have been the check engine light—something that can be ignored, at least for a while. In this case, apparently it could not be ignored.

"There's a house over there," said Myrtle Gawp. "Maybe we can plug into an outlet in their garage or something."

"Well, um," Figgy stuttered. "I need to find a DC power source for a quick charge. I—well, I guess I could have brought my adapter, but then you're looking at 20 hours to charge."

"And where do we find this DC power source?" I asked.

"Usually in big cities," Figgy said.

We were of course 300 miles from a big city. In fact, we were somewhere on a road with no name looking for something enormous and sweet per our latest Road Rally clue. I, of course, felt there was nothing greater and sweeter than serving God, but was told in no uncertain terms that I was on the wrong track. Therefore, we were

headed to some bakery. Except we took a wrong turn onto "no name" road and were running low on juice.

"There's a plug at the waterfront in Budworm," Figgy said. "If we make it."

## Team Maki

"I thought you said that Toivo fixed the leak in the gas tank," Evi said as the Maki cousins coasted to a stop along the side of US 41, just shy of the looming statue that dominated an overlook high above them.

"He did," Tami snapped, "but it was a temporary fix. Besides, the gas gauge doesn't work, so maybe it emptied of—natural causes."

"I told you I smelled gas on our way down the mountain," Evi said. "Hope nobody tosses a cigarette out their window."

"Well, there's nothing to do but get the gas can out of the back—but first we need to re-repair the leak," Tami said, giving Evi a meaningful look.

"Why me!" It's your dumb truck. I mean, who has a utility pole for a bumper?

"It got us through that brush, didn't it?" Tami said.

"True enough," Evi said. "Of course, the road was only ten feet away and we wouldn't have *needed* to bushwhack if yous had just taken the *@$#* road. Probably that bramble thicket tore off the *@&#* gas tank patch."

"It was a shortcut," Tami snapped.

"Sure. A shortcut to hel—"

"Here's the Ape Tape," Tami said shoving an enormous roll of black tape at her cousin. "You're the mechanical genius—go fix what my wingnut husband screwed up."

Evi sighed and took the roll of tape.

## Team Nettie Bramble

"We're not gonna make it!"

The whining noise coming from the other side of the truck was just my two nephews, Wanton and Wiley. They were part of the deal for me getting the Honey Wagon for the road rally.

"Pa says that when you have a full load, you gotta avoid going up and down steep hills, because the engine *and* the brakes need some work."

We were halfway up some goat path trying to find some clue at the top of some mountain, except we weren't gonna make it to the top carrying a few thousand gallons of sewage. Even with the gas pedal crammed to the floor, we were only going about a mile an hour. I even saw a turtle pass us. I swear he gave me a smug look to boot.

"Okay, out!" I snarled. "This calls for desperate measures!"

"But us getting out isn't going to help," said Wanton.

"I gotta go!" said Wiley. I swear that kid's never gonna have Kool Aid again on my watch.

"Now, Wanton, you get your brother outa the way while I let go some of this weight," I said, as I headed back to the sewage tank emptying gizmo.

"You have to hook on the hose!" Wanton said, "so's you can direct the flow. Hey, I see a bunch of trucks and cars coming!"

"Hose, smoze. How hard could it be to just give a little turn and let go some of th—"

"Holy crackers!" yelled Wanton.

"Waaaaaaaaaaa!" Come from the youngest who didn't get outa the way in time.

Good thing was that the cars and trucks behind us were running in the Road Rally and they wouldn't be getting up to the clue at the top of the mountain any time soon.

### Team Bea

"At least the Fun Bus don't have to be plugged in," said Myrtle, as she looked over my shoulder. "I didn't know you could drive this thing."

"Of course I can," I said. We had exchanged the useless Tezzlala for the Gnarly Woods Senior Complex "Fun Bus," which Figgy had the Gnarly Complex manager, Elwood Fuddy, bring out to us at the intersection of Nowhere and Noplace. They used some kind of global hunting gadget to work it out. Figgy and Fuddy stayed with the Tezzlala waiting for the local wrecker, Buzz's Towing, to show up. The "dispatcher" (Buzz's wife) said she'd track him down, probably drinking beer at the American Legion.

## Team Maki

"Bad news," Evi said as she crawled out from under Big Buck and hoisted herself up.

"Didn't you fix the gas tank?" Tami said, poised by the gas cap of the truck ready with the backup gas can that went wherever Big Buck went.

"Sure—I patched all SEVEN leaks—we may have added some in the briar patch. The bad news is the oil leak."

"Ah," said Tami, as she glugged fuel into the truck. "So, is it around the gasket or is there a hole in the pan?"

"Huh?" Evi said. Since when did her cousin sound so auto mechanical savvy?

"I just asked what kind of oil leak," Tami said, putting the empty can back into the bed of the truck.

"A bad one," Evi responded. "The kind that happens when your so-called oil pan no longer exists."

"What!" Tami said.

"Again, likely a victim of our bushwhacking. It's hanging by one rusty bolt. I have no idea why the engine didn't just—well, stop."

Actually, it had *just stopped*. Tami had assumed it was the gas leak. Perhaps not. Tami got out her phone and called Buzzy's Towing. His wife said he was on another call somewhere in the boonies.

## Team Nettie

"Look what I found up there at the top!" said Wiley.

He shoved something in my face that looked like a throw-away lighter, and he about burned off my eyebrow. Ma used to have one to light her pipe.

"Get ridda that thing," I snapped at Wiley. "You don't need cigarettes to stunt your growth.

"But it won't shut off," he whined.

We had made it to the top and were now headed back down, which was like one of those obstacle courses what with dodging all the vehicles that had slid into the ditch—or worse—on account of maybe a little slippery sewage discharge on the road. I had all I could do keeping the Honey Wagon from joining the others in the ditch—or worse—on account of brakes that come and go like a summer breeze.

"I said git rid of that thing before yous set us all on fire!"

"Okay—don't yell at me," Wiley said, tossing the lighter out the window.

We were picking up speed, which was good, when we hear a kind of WHOOOSH.

"Wow!" said the boys, looking out the window. "That was cool!

### Team Bea

It was the Christian thing to do—to offer a ride. My heavens, I had no idea it would mean that they would become part of the Righteous team. However, I owed the Maki cousins a favor, since they had saved me from a very unsavory situation back some time ago in Sin City, where, while on a mission from God, I had been blessed with an enormous jackpot at the slots. Before the bells and whistles could even stop, I was beckoned into the dark sanctum of Boss Bosco's office, and it soon became clear that Boss had no intention of paying up. That was, until the Maki women made a colossal scene and justice prevailed.

"So, we can share the winnings," said Evi Maki, as she leaned over my shoulder. Blessedly, we were *finally* headed for the last clue. Something to do with a "treasure hidden right under our nose." More gibberish, which did not bode well with me as we headed out Ghost River Road.

"Like heck!" said Myrtle. "This here is our gig. Yous are just along for the ride!"

"We can offer a substantial discount for six months at our Wickiup Fudge and Wine Shoppe in exchange," offered Tami.

Wine! Indeed!

"Now yer talkin'," said Myrtle. "That place is the bees' trees."

"Knees," I corrected.

"Huh?"

"Turn here!" Evi said. "This is Ghost River Road!"

The Fun Bus squealed a bit at the abrupt turn, then spewed a plume of dust as it sped down the dirt road.

### Team Nettie

"My feet hurt!" whined the youngest. "I'm hungry, too."

"You ate a whole giant sweet roll," said the oldest.

"Yeah, but it didn't stick with me," said the youngest.

"You're a pig!"

"Am not!"

"Oink! Oink! Oink!!"

"Waaaaaaa!"

"SHUT UP!" I said.

See, me and the boys had to go ahead and get outa the Honey Wagon on account of the fire. I had thought I'd smelled gas on the way up, and now thinking about it, I should never have told Wiley to throw out that lighter. Anyhow, it was like something from a horror movie with a fiery scene that traps everyone. But we got out, because there was a crick running long side the road and I saved us and the Honey Wagon by driving into it. Except the truck got caught up in a kind of deep spot, and the engine just quit. This wasn't no sparkling little crick, either, maybe because there was some spill from when I let go the innards of the Honey Wagon on the way up.

Anyways, we were hoofing it to our last clue. I knew from huntin' the area that the ol' ski trail would lead to Ghost River Road where some kinda treasure was hid. Maybe we could hitch a ride.

"Hey! There's a road!" shouted Wanton.

"Someone's coming!" shouted Wiley.

Nobody's gonna just leave a lone woman and two kids stranded, so we waved our arms and a sawed-off bus skidded to a dusty stop about two inches from us.

### Team Bea, et. al

"Did anybody think to bring a shovel?"

This was asked by Tami Maki, since the next and final clue seemed to indicate hidden treasure. Traditionally, treasure was buried and we surmised that a shovel might be a needed tool.

"There's a snow shovel next to the spare tire in the compartment under the bus," said Myrtle with her first useful comment of the day.

"Me and the boys appreciate you pickin' us up," said that dreadful Bramble woman. I remembered Ms. Bramble from the Prom Bomb at the Gnarly Woods Senior Complex. She was in charge of activities as part of her community service to fulfill a court-ordered requirement for some illegitimate shenanigans involving a deer carcass.

"We are good at digging up worms!" shouted one of the little urchins that accompanied the Bramble woman.

"Aunt Nettie wants to put a toilet in her cabin!" added the other boy.

Worms and toilets. Lovely. And I must say the threesome positively reeked. Perhaps helping this backwoods trio obtain a source of running water in order to bathe would be a charitable act indeed.

"What does No Outlet mean?" asked the older boy.

"Means dead end," said Myrtle. "I danced to a band once that was called The Dead End. We were hot!"

"And here we are at the dead end," I said, stopping the bus *and* Myrtle, lest she go into more details about her life as a rock star.

"So, we need to read the clue again," said Myrtle.

"But we looked on the way here, and they're not all the same," said Tami Maki.

"Okay. Clues—plural," said Evi Maki. "Who's first?"

"Wanton," piped up the Bramble woman. "Read everyone our clue."

Wanton had to go through all his pockets and finally found a bedraggled slip of paper that had their clue.

"Okay, but it's dumb," he said unfolding the grubby piece of paper.

> *Put them together and it will help you in finding,*
> *a basic lesson of which bears reminding.*

"He's right," said Myrtle, "it doesn't make sense."

"Now wait a moment," I said. "Myrtle, read ours."

"Okay," she said clearing her throat. She also had to search the pockets of her cardigan sweater for a moment and pulled out first her reading glasses and then a folded piece of paper.

> *That working together will pay over time,*
> *great riches for all just watch for the sign.*

Well, my heavens, I had been so caught up in the blasted road rally, I had been negligent in keeping my spiritual radar in tune for a "sign" from the Lord. Clearly, the devil had been at the wheel, steering me away from my duty as moral compass for this venture.

The Maki cousins looked befuddled and Tami said, "I don't think our clue will help one iota. But go ahead, Evi. Read it."

Evi pulled her crumpled piece of paper from somewhere in the depths of her ample bosom and smoothed it out. She squinted, then turned the paper around.

> *The end of the road is only the start,*
> *the clue that each has is only one part.*

"Well, that clears things up," Tami said sarcastically.

The two boys started assaulting one another, so I opened the Fun Bus door and everyone piled out. We stood on the dusty road looking for enlightenment.

"Skeeters are suckin' me dry!" said Nettie Bramble, swatting the air around her.

"Hey," Myrtle said. "Someone take my picture here at the Dead End sign. I'm gonna FaceNook it and see if any of the peeps from the band are still alive and remember how we shook our booty in them days!"

"Wait a minute!" Evi Maki said. "The sign! It says watch for the sign. Gimme the shovel!"

Turns out a snow shovel does not work well in hard-packed earth.

"There's no SIGN of any disturbed earth here," Tami Maki said to her cousin. "If someone had buried the so-called treasure, we would see some SIGN of it."

Then I, Bea Righteous, had an epiphany. Angel voices filled the air and the sun came from beneath some ominous black clouds and illuminated the dust motes floating about.

"Kindly give me all the clues," I said, holding out my hand.

"How come?" asked Tami Maki.

"Just please let me do something," I said.

So, everyone handed me their soiled clue papers.

"Aha!" said Myrtle, peering down at them.

"Aha, what?" Evi Maki said.

"Nothin'," said Myrtle. "I just always wanted to say that. Aha!"

"Ah, but now we are getting somewhere," I said. "They need to be arranged in order."

> *The end of the road is only the start,*

*the clue that each has is only one part.*
*Put them together and it will help you in finding,*
*a basic lesson of which bears reminding.*
*That working together will pay over time,*
*great riches for all, just watch for the sign.*

"Okay, now we're back to the sign," said Tami Maki.

"Well, maybe there's a clue taped on the back or somthin'," said Nettie Bramble.

We inspected every square inch of the sign and just found some graffiti spray painted on the back.

"I didn't know they had gangs out here in the sticks," said Myrtle. "Looky here, some gang bangers calling themselves The Road Rages."

"There's something else," Nettie said.

*Justice for all! It will do you no harm,*
*go visit the courthouse and find three's the charm.*

"Three's the charm?" Tami said.

"Well, there were three clues to get here," I said.

"And we were originally three teams," Evi said.

"Justice," Nettie said. "Ol' Judge Nightshade is on the third floor of the courthouse. I just as soon not ask him about any prize."

"But the treasurer is on the third floor too!" said Tami. "Let's go!"

Well, so much for a spiritual sign. Everyone piled into the Fun Bus and I did a twenty- point turn and finally got us pointed back around and we headed for the courthouse, though I certainly felt it was an unlikely final destination. And there was still the little matter of who was entitled to the prize money.

A very sour looking woman with a pointy nose and rhinestone glasses dangling from a chain around her neck inspected us as we piled into the treasurer's office, each trying to elbow one another aside so we'd be first in line.

"Well, well," said Pointy Nose. "Looks like you all are the first to figure out that ridiculously easy road rally adventure." She cleared her throat. "Of course, I do believe that there may have been some cheating, as I heard something about a sewage spill and a fire on the mountain. Four fire departments are on the scene, along with the EPA.

You wouldn't know anything about what may have happened, would you?" she asked, looking pointedly at each of us.

"Yeah, it was—ow!" said Wiley

"Shut up," said Wanton.

"Well, it certainly eliminated some competition," said Pointy Nose. "Now, then, about the prize money."

I cleared my throat. "As you can see—" I peered at her name tag partially obscured by her glasses chain.

"Miss Beakie," supplied the woman.

"Anyway, Miss Beakie," I said. "It may be difficult to determine how to fairly divide the prize money among all of us."

"It should be in thirds," said Tami Maki. "Three's the charm, right?"

"Well, yes," said Miss Beakie. "But you solved the BIG clue—more like the key to unity and harmony."

"Huh?" said Nettie Bramble. "The key to what?"

"You see, the object of the Road Rally was to get people in the community to work TOGETHER, and therefore each team needed to connect with other teams to take this thing to the home stretch."

"Cool!" said Wanton and Wiley together, which was the first time I had witnessed them in agreement during this whole ordeal.

"So, cut the doodoo, Beakie. What's the plan?" Myrtle never was one to mince words.

"Well," said Beakie with a sniff, "not only will each original team get five thousand dollars, but you will ALL have a plaque made in your honor and hung in the town hall. You, dear people, are the only contestants to have figured out that you needed to be ONE team, pulling in the right direction. It aligns with our village motto, you know."

"Village motto?" I queried. I did not know of a village motto for Budworm, though I had heard many unsavory nicknames over the years, such as Earworm, Wormville, Bugburg, etc.

"Budworm! ONE community ONE mind ONE fine place," said Miss Beakie. "Go Crawlers!" she added. That was the school "team" name: The Night Crawlers. The school mascot, though meant to emulate a giant worm and who bore the nickname "Wormy" more resembled a hot dog that had been on the gas station rotisserie too long. The simulated earth clumps crumbled on his back looked suspiciously like chili sauce sprinkled with onions.

Well, my heavens, but it had been a very long day and we all had an overwhelming urge to have chili cheese hot dogs—perhaps triggered by the mental vision of "Wormy." So, the Gnarly Woods Fun Bus pulled into the root beer stand (yes, Budworm still had one). The squabbling began when we tried to figure out who owed for what when the check arrived. So much for unity and harmony.

~ ~ ~

*Did you figure out the clues?*
*1. Mount Arvon (Michigan's Highest Point)*
*2. Bishop Baraga Shrine (The Legendary Snowshoe Priest)*
*3. Hilltop Restaurant (Home of the Famous Sweet Roll)*

# The Bramble Beast

Ma was asleep in front of the TV and I was working on getting the snarl out of my fishing line so's I could hit my secret fishin' spot before it got too hot and buggy. Tick season was almost over but the skeeters were still fat and sassy. Darned if I could figure out how my tackle got so blasted tangled up. I suspected it had something to do with my two pain-in-the-patootie nephews.

Speak of the devil—or maybe spawn of the devil—if those two rascals didn't come busting into the cabin making enough racket to raise the dead.

"What th'—!" Ma screeched, jumpin' outa her recliner and dumpin' her supposed cup of coffee on her slippers.

Myself, I had almost gotten the last knot out of my fishing line when the invasion of the rug rats made me drop the whole getup, and the reel just kept spittin' out line that went everywhere.

Next to come in was my Perfect Sister and her pudden-head husband, Tag. He was moving slow and made a clumpin' noise every other step.

I was chasing fishing line all over the floor and my nephews got down to help, and like you'd probably figure, just made things worse.

"Hey! Watch it boys," I said, "there's still—"

"Owwww! Waaaaaa," shrieked Wiley.

"—a hook," I said.

"You're such a sissy pants!" said Wanton.

"Am not!"

"Are too!"

"Don't call your brother names," MarshMarigold said.

Tag thumped his way over to the fridge, pulled open the door, and stuck his head in.

"Shut yer yaps!" Ma yelled. "C'mere and Granny will pull that hook out." She looked at Tag. "What in blazes'd you do to yer foot?"

"Tell her, Tag," M&M said.

"Nuthin," Tag said. "You got any Coke?"

"In fronta yer face!" Ma said.

"Dad got a cast on his foot because he got mad at the Honey Wagon," Wanton said. "He said a bad word."

A blood-curdling scream gave us all a jolt. I'd almost had the line back on the dang reel, and it let loose again, jumping around like a jack rabbit.

"Nothin' to it," Ma said holding up a hook that either had a piece of dried-up worm on it or maybe a chunk of Wiley's thumb.

MarshMarigold pulled a Band-Aid out of her purse and patched up the boy's thumb. "Now you've got to be brave if you're going camping with Aunt Nettie."

"Wha—camping?" I said.

"I wanna know what numbnuts over there done to his foot!" Ma said.

"Blasted truck was acting up," Tag said. "The valve was stuck—again. I fixed it so many times…"

"Dad kicked the truck and broke his foot!" Wanton said.

"I don't wanna go camping!" Wiley said.

"Good, 'cause I'm not gonna take you," I said.

"I have to go!" Wanton shouted. "So I can go out on a limb. Pleeeessssee!"

"Out on a limb?" I said.

"Here's the deal," M&M said. "Wanton needs to spend a night, er, rustic camping, cooking out, lashing things, sleeping in a tent and whatnot so he can earn his Fun in the Forest Badge. He needs the badge to *grow* from Seedling status to Sapling in the Tree Hugger Kids Club, or just Huggers for short. They call the different badges branches of the tree and the adventure is having the kids—or tree huggers—going out on a limb. His father was going to take him, but Mr. Potty Mouth—"

"Yeah, they get the picture," Tag said.

"Anyway," she said, "it's like a scout troop, only they've, er, updated it. We figured Wiley should go too, since it would be a good way for him to, um, toughen up a little."

"He's such a sissy pants," Wanton said.

"AM NOT!" Wiley said.

"SHUT UP! Both of you," I said.

"What'n hell comes after sapling?" Ma said. She had refilled and topped off her "coffee" and was sitting down in front of the TV, which she had muted.

"Mature," M&M said. "Something that's a long way off. Anyway, see, the Tree Hugger Kids Club is for boys and girls. They wanted to get away from things like Brownie, Tenderfoot, Cub, Eagle, and Cadet. So when the kids achieve *growth* they give them names such as Sprout, Seedling, Sapling and so on."

"Why?" Ma said.

"Um...I guess because it's woodsy and gender-neutral."

"Gender wha'?" Ma said, taking a sip from her cup.

"I gotta go this weekend," Wanton whined. "The banquet is almost here."

M&M sighed. "The Huggers have a banquet every year and the kids get their badges."

"I got one last year!" shouted Wiley.

"Yes you did, sweetie. A participation badge. Because he, um, showed up."

Ma snorted. "Big deal!"

"Well, it's a start for our little Sprout. So, what do you say, Nettie? The boys must have an adult supervising, and I'd go, but I have an unavoidable scheduling conflict. And you're so—outdoorsy!" she said.

"What's in it for me?" I muttered, looking gloomily at the hopeless snarl of fishing line.

"You name it!" M&M said.

I couldn't pass on that offer. I told my Perfect Sister to warm up her charge card and went to fetch my fishing catalog. I'd seen her order stuff on her fancy smart phone, and I figured a nice new rod, reel, and a few extras would be a fair exchange for babysitting a couple of spoiled brats.

\* \* \*

"This here's a perfect spot," I said. "Dump the gear over there."

"But Aunt Nettie," whined Wanton, "it's just the gravel pit behind your place. I can still see the cabin."

"Darn tootin'," I said. "No sense in hauling all this stuff halfway across the county. Now get the tent out and we'll set up camp."

Well, the boys no more had an idea how to pitch a tent than to build an ark, so I had to mostly do the settin' up while they fought over who got to pound in the stakes using a big rock, since we forgot a hammer. Stakes all popped out anyway and I had to set them right.

"Now get your stuff put inside and zip up the door before the skeeters get in," I said, slapping at one of the little buggers on the back of my neck.

"Hey, Aunt Nettie," said the youngest, "where's your sleeping bag?"

"Don't need one," I said.

"How come?" said the oldest.

"Because I don't plan on bunking with you two popcorn farts," I said.

"Where you gonna sleep?" Wanton asked.

"Don't worry about that right now," I said. "Now we'll start off having a blast with a Paul Bunyan hike."

"What's a Paul Bunyan hike?" Wiley asked.

"Well, you hike out in the woods and collect up some firewood," I said. What self-respecting kid didn't know what a Paul Bunyan hike was? Or a snipe hunt, for that matter.

Both kids looked at me like I had worms crawling out of my ears.

"What do we do with all that wood?" said Wanton.

"Yeah, there's bugs and icky stuff in the woods!" whined Wiley.

"You make a fire and cook your supper on it," I said.

I hadn't thought 'til then that the only fire they ever had was in their la-de-da gas firepit on their deck. You'd have thought that being a club about trees, that someone woulda taught them what collecting firewood meant. But apparently hugging trees and burnin' parts of them's two different things. The to-do list that my sister gave me said we had to cook over a campfire.

"Fires are dangerous!" said Wanton.

"All the bugs will die in the fire!" sniveled Wiley. "I don't wanna kill the bugs."

"Oh for crying out loud!" I said. "We'll give the bugs a warning before we set the fire. Now go and get us some wood."

"Aunt Nettie?"

"What now, Wanton?" I snapped.

"Why don't we just go back to the cabin and get firewood you got stacked there?"

"Because," I said, "that's for heatin' the cabin next winter, not to mess around with a couple of spikehorns like you two."

"Then can you drive us to the store?" he said.

"What th' heck for?" I said. We already had all the makings for tinfoil dinners, s'mores, campfire pies, and wieners on a stick."

"So we can buy some firewood!" he said. "I've seen wood all shrink-wrapped and stacked at the store and says it's $6.99 a bundle."

Best idea the kid had ever had, especially since we used his money. We also picked up a can of lighter fluid, which works a whole lot better than soggy pine needles. Since firewood was expensive, we figured it was cheaper to buy us some sub sandwiches, chips, and a box of those little cupcakes along with a few Bucking Bronco energy drinks to wash it all down. That would save the firewood for the weenie roast and s'mores.

When we got back to the campsite, I looked at the "to do" list. "Says here we got to dig a latrine," I said.

"What's a latrine?" Wanton said.

"A hole in the ground that you use like a privy, except it's got no walls," I said.

"Ewwwww!" squealed Wiley.

"Yeah, but Aunt Nettie, the outhouse to the cabin is just over there," Wanton said, pointing to the little square building about 100 feet downwind from us.

"Good point," I said crossing "latrine" off the list. "We'll just dig a hole and throw our trash in it then cover it up, so's you can practice."

The boys set off about two feet away from camp and dug a hole in the gravel using a tin plate, since we'd forgot a shovel.

"Okay," I said. "Next thing is to do some lashin'. Go get that ball of twine from the truck, Wiley, and try not to trip over the tent stakes again."

"What's lashing, Aunt Nettie?" Wanton said, grabbing the ball of twine from his brother.

"It's when you tie things together," I said. "Don't they teach you anything in that tree bugger club?"

"Tree HUGGER!" said Wanton.

"Why in heck would anyone want to hug a tree?" I said.

Both boys shrugged their shoulders. I wondered what they were teaching kids these days—hugging trees and calling themselves tree names and whatnot, instead of coming up with good nicknames like Fatty Four-Eyes and Slimy Slug Sam.

"Wanton, go tie the end of this twine on that tree branch over there," I said.

"Why?" he said.

"I told you. We're doing some lashin'," I said.

"But aren't we supposed to make a table or something like that?" Wanton said.

"This will be a clothesline," I said, "once we get both ends tied to trees."

"What do we need a clothesline for?" Wiley said.

"To dry your clothes, sleeping bags, and the tent," I said.

"Mommy just puts stuff in the clothes dryer," Wiley said.

"Besides," said Wanton, "our stuff isn't wet."

I looked at the ugly black clouds off to the west. "It will be. Anyway, it's almost time to turn in."

"But Aunt Nettie," said Wanton, "it's only 5:30!"

"Right—well, see, yous want to be tucked in before the Bramble Beast comes wanderin' through," I said. "So, we best get the campfire going so's we can check that off the list before *dark*."

"Br-br-bramble Beast?" Wiley said.

"Yup," I said. "We call him BB for short. I'll keep watch, though. Nothing to worry about. Now stand back while I give this wood a good squirt of starter."

The fire lit with a whoosh and flames shot up about six feet before they settled into a smoky sizzle.

"Now get your marshmallows going, boys. Times a wasting," I said, giving a glance off across the gravel pit. "I know the BB has his den somewhere in the pit, so I'll keep a lookout."

"I wanna go home!" Wiley said.

"Sissy pants!" said Wanton. "I don't believe in any ol' Bramble Beast. You just made that up, Aunt Nettie."

"Ya think so, eh?" I said, giving the boy a hard look. "What you think those claw marks are on the privy over there?"

"Maybe it was a bear," Wanton said.

"Maybe, maybe not," I said. "Of course a bear can do a boy a lot of harm if it finds he don't go to bed by dark."

"Take me home!" sniveled you-know-who.

"Naw, yous'll be fine," I said, just as a low rumble of thunder came through the camp.

"What was that!" Wiley shrieked.

"What—I didn't hear—oh that. It was just the ol' BB in his den. Probably still sleeping and snoring some. He won't come out 'til after dark, and we got us at least ten minutes until the rain—er nighttime."

The sky turned real dark and ugly and it was like someone turned off the lights.

"Let's go ahead and bury our trash in the latrine, boys, and yous need to get in your sleeping bags," I said. A couple of fat raindrops hit me in the face.

"We gotta put the fire out!" Wanton said. "We could start a forest fire."

I looked at the sky. The rain was picking up. "I don't think you need to worry about that," I said.

When a pretty big clap of thunder came, the boys ran each other over scrambling to get in the tent. Myself, I figured I'd just climb up in the cab of my truck and nap there until the boys got scared out of their pants and we'd all go back to the cabin. I'd give them about an hour. Or maybe one would need the outhouse but be afraid to go alone. I admit the rain pitter patter kind of lulled me to sleep, and thunder and a little lightnin' never hurt nobody. At least not usually. Anyway, I drifted off for longer than I thought I would and when I came to, I thought I'd get out of the truck and check on the boys. I unzipped the flap and poked my head in. Those kids were sound asleep. I slipped inside, hoping to wake them and maybe they'd beg to go back to the cabin.

Then there was a real strange noise.

Splut, slosh, splut, slosh…

"What the…?" I said, accidentally on purpose waking up the boys.

Splut, slosh, splut, slosh—It was getting closer!

"What's that!" Wanton said.

The youngest rubbed his eyes and went into a snivel fit about the Bramble Beast.

"Okay boys," I whispered. "We're gonna be real quiet. Probably just an ol' porcupine or skunk or something sniffing around the latrine."

Splut, slosh, splut, slosh—Ahhhhhhhh!!!!

That wasn't a little critter.

"Come on boys," I shouted, "make a run for the truck!" I grabbed each of 'em by the arm and we flew outa that tent, barely touching the ground. We dove into the truck, and I cranked her up and threw it in gear. Mud flew everywhere from spinning the tires. We got back to the cabin in record time and all sat in the truck for a minute to catch our breath.

"Hey, that's our car," Wanton said pointing to the Alder SUV parked near the cabin.

When we got inside, we expected to see MarshMarigold and Tag sitting around waiting for us to chicken out. Except nobody was there besides Ma snoring from her bedroom off the kitchen. The TV and all the lights were off.

I grabbed a flashlight and shotgun and decided to sneak back to the campsite to find out what the heck made that weird noise. When I got there, my bro-in-law was lying in a puddle with the twine clothesline wrapped every which way around him. The cast on his foot was sunk deep in the mud.

I put my flashlight in his face. He blinked away a bunch of mud and gave me his hand so I could pull him up.

"I was just checking on you guys," Tag said. "You know, make sure the boys were okay with all the rain and everything. I forgot a flashlight."

I glanced over at the soggy, drooping tent. It looked as if it might be starting to float.

"You don't need to, er, tell them?" Tag said. "I'll just take the boys home, and not let on I was checking up on you. Or that some damn thing snagged me and I fell on my face in the mud."

I looked him over then smiled. "Well, the way I see it," I said, "is that you came by to drop off something real important, like a hammer—since we had to use a rock to pound in the tent stakes—and then see this big nasty creature, we'll call it the Bramble Beast, about to tear into the boy's tent and you give chase and run the bugger off, maybe using the hammer."

"You'd do that for me?" Tag said.

"You betcha. Of course I'm thinking that it sure would be nice to have a new tackle box to go with that rod 'n reel MarshMarigold ordered…"

## Flying Blind

Ma was sitting in front of
her TV watching her "soaps"
while I was trying to figure out
how to build a duck blind out on
the state land without being spotted.
Building a blind wasn't the problem and
hiding from ducks wasn't the problem.
Problem was that all the good huntin' spots
was where CO Will Ketchum prowled around
checking licenses and bag limits and whatnot.

"What I need is to get one of them duck blind
boats," I said, picking up my Crooked Rod Adventure Catalog.

"Getcha wha?" Ma said, takin' a sip of her whiskied-up coffee. She
called it her eye opener, but far as I can tell it mostly conks her out.

"A duck boat," I said. "You get a camo flat-bottom boat and fix it
up with weeds and twigs and build a floating blind. Not only could I
fool the ducks, but also Will Ketchum. I build a regular duck blind in
the cattails, and he's gonna sniff me out in a day. But if I could poke
around in my duck blind boat, I'd just look like a patch of pond weeds
floating in the current."

"Humph," Ma said. "So quit blabbin' about it and get one of them
things. I could go for some of my chicken-fried duck."

"Costs a bundle," I said as I thumbed through my catalog. I could
maybe afford a couple of camo decals to stick on the side. That was
about it.

Ma snorted and said, "So get a dang huntin' license and maybe
Ketchum will die of shock when you whip it out to show 'em."

It was a matter of principle that I didn't get a license of any kind—
huntin', fishin', drivin', or otherwise. Don't pay parking tickets either

and sure as heck don't leave a tip for someone just for bringing me a beer.

"Thing is, these duck boats are nothing but rafts with sides and a motor stuck on the back," I said to Ma who was nodding off, so I guess I said it more to myself. Before I could give myself an answer, my two nephews come banging into the cabin causing Ma to yelp and spill her "coffee."

"Dang it!" Ma said dabbing a napkin at the coffee/booze on her shirt. "I jist washed this last week. Don't you brats ever knock?"

"Mommy said we could spend the day with Aunt Nettie!" said Wiley.

"Yeah," said Wanton. "She and Dad have got to haul some stuff to the dump, and said we had to stay here."

"How come yous two lint balls can't go to the dump?" Ma said.

"Because," Wanton said, giving Wiley an ugly look, "crybaby here fell in the thing last time and almost got smushed."

"Fell in what?" I said.

"You know, that big pit where you dump stuff and then it gets all crushed up and, I don't know, taken away and buried or something," Wanton said. "It was totally cool! Wiley smelled real bad and the man running the place said us kids couldn't come back. Anyway, Dad tore down some old wood outhouses at the park and the toilet company put up some new plastic ones and they paid Dad to haul off the wood and stuff and he and Mom are taking it—"

Before the kid could finish I was out the door flagging down MarshMarigold and Tag before they could pull away. After I picked through the boards, tin roof parts, and whatnot, I had most all I needed to make a duck blind raft. The only thing missing was some cheap labor and maybe a couple of paddles. I looked over my nephews and shrugged. They'd have to do.

"Is this going to be like Tom Sawyer's raft?" Wiley asked.

"Kinda," I said. Now hold that board still while I nail the cross piece."

"WAAAAAA! You pounded my thumb!"

"Told you to hold it still," I snapped. "Suck on your thumb and it'll be good as new."

We finally got about ten decent boards nailed side by side by attaching them to crosspieces. Then we put some old roof tin over the contraption for a floor and lashed a frame out of branches to give a place to attach the blind makings.

"You boys go fetch a bunch of twigs and willow shoots and leaves—whatever you can haul and we'll weave them into the frame, then we'll put the whole caboodle in the back of the truck."

The thing weighed a ton, but we got her up in the bed of my truck. I tossed in a couple of canoe paddles that were held together with duct tape and some wood poles that Tag was supposed to use to make me and Ma a clothesline. They'd been sitting around for three years along with the rope waiting for Tag to get some gumption.

"You two get your butts in the truck and I'll go tell Granny that we're going for a test ride in this contraption."

"I wanna give it a name," Wiley said. "You know, like Uncle Willie's fishing boat that he calls the Wandering Willie."

Willie Alder was Tag's older brother. Ma said that the two of them shared a brain, whatever the heck that means.

"Let's name it the Bramble Blind!" Wanton blurted out.

"No!" whined Wiley. "I think it should be the Alder Blind."

"Call it whatever you want," I said. "If we don't wanna miss supper, we need to git."

In the interest of saving time, I decided we'd launch the Bramble Blind or whatever it's called at the nearest body of water for a quick test. Turns out the Sisu River was the closest. Since it hadn't rained in a while, I figured the river would be slow and easy and we'd have us a nice float. I mighta figured wrong. Anyway, I brought my Magic Quacker and my shotgun along with some shells I put in my pocket just in case we saw any ducks. Always smart to be ready.

I backed the truck down the boat ramp as far as I could. The ride had done a number on the twigs, shoots, and leaves and we had to make some repairs. Once we got the thing put back together, me and the boys dragged the Bramble Blind down into the shallow water and give her a good push.

"Well poke me with a stick and call me done," I said. "The thing's floating just as pretty as can be."

"Hey, wait a minute," said Wanton. "How do we get back after we go down the river?"

"The tide," I said.

"Whaaa?" said Wiley.

"The Sisu's got a kind of tide that makes it go backwards 'bout every 45 minutes, or maybe it's 35 minutes. Anyhow, we'll time it so's we can go with the tide and float on back to the truck, slick as can be."

"I thought only oceans had tides," said Wanton, looking at the raft that might have been sitting a little cockeyed.

"Nope," I said. "Now buckle on the life jackets and grab ahold so we can catch the current going out."

Me and the boys scrambled up, kind of tipping the thing for a minute. She righted herself okay but drifted out into the river before we could get settled. Since the raft didn't have a rudder or a keel to keep it going frontways, the Bramble Blind switched off going frontways, then sideways, then backwards.

"Get the paddles and start using them!" I shouted to the boys. Of course they had no more an idea of how to use a canoe paddle on a raft than how to dress out a deer.

We were going every which way for a while then the river smoothed out, which was good, except we couldn't steer the thing worth a toot and was heading right for a rocky island smack in the middle of the river.

"I gotta pee!" Wiley said, dancing around and making the raft bounce.

"Okay, okay. Hold yer horses. We're headed for that sandbar off the island. We can land there and you can go use the woods and we'll wait for the tide to kick in."

The raft scraped bottom, turned clean around, dug in, and jerked to a stop on the sand bar.

"I figure we got about ten minutes before the tide lifts us off this sandbar and sends us on back to the truck. Or maybe five minutes."

"I really gotta go!" whined Wiley.

"Well, hop out and take care of it," I snapped. "Now you got nine minutes, or maybe four minutes."

Just as Wiley jumped onto the sandbar, there was a rustle in the trees along the shore and out stepped CO Will Ketchum.

"Well, well, well," he said. "What do we have here, Bramble?"

"I gotta go!" Wiley shouted, racing past Ketchum into the brush.

"Wow!" said Wanton. "It's the woods cop. Do you have your gun?"

"Question is," said Ketchum, "do YOU have a gun?" He was looking at me.

"You bet," I said. "I wouldn't head out on a river ride without my gun. There's wolves and bears and all sorts of things looking to make a meal outa a couple of kids."

"Uh, huh," Ketchum said, looking our raft over. He walked around it clucking his tongue. "What in Sam Hill is this thing?"

"This here is a river raft. Me and the boys are, ah…"

"Playing Tom Sawyer!" piped up Wanton. I was proud of the boy for being so quick on his feet.

"And this pile of shi—er *debris* is…?" said Ketchum.

"A duck—er, dinosaur blind. So's we can hide from flying dinosaurs!" Wanton said.

I was beginning to think there was hope for this kid. He had a lot of Bramble bull in him.

Just then Wiley comes back from the woods, still zipping up. "Dinosaurs!" he shrieked, running into the blind. Next we know, the little hooligan has found my Magic Quacker and starts to blat on it.

"It's a dinosaur caller," I said, giving Ketchum a big grin and wink.

"Riiiight," he said.

I looked at my watch. "We got about five minutes—maybe less—Ketchum, then we gotta catch the tide back to where we come from."

"Tide? You got booze in there or something?" he said, giving the raft a little nudge with his toe.

"You know, the Sisu reverses and we need to get off this sandbar in (I checked my watch) about two minutes."

"Well, not 'til I look around and make sure there's no contraband on this thing," he said.

"Huh?" said Wanton. "Hey, we're floating!"

We sure were, and just like I said, we were headed upstream, with the Bramble Blind making good headway, even though it was spinning in a slow circle. I tried to use a paddle as a kind of rudder to control it but wasn't having much luck.

"Hey!" shouted Ketchum. "Let me off this piece of—!"

"Too late," I said. "Told you there was a tide coming, but you had to sniff around. Now grab that other paddle and help me steer this thing!"

"Bramble, I don't know what law you're breaking, but I'll find one and Judge Nightshade will throw the book at you!"

"Oh yeah?" I said. "Looks to me like you are a stowaway on this vessel. Now, if you're real nice and help us load it when we get back to my truck, I won't tell what happened to your boss—what's her name again?"

"You mean my wife?" Ketchum said, while he churned the water into a froth with his paddle. "Why are we going so fast?"

"No, not your wife, the other boss lady. Wanda something. Stern—that's it, Wanda Stern, your supervisor. She and I were pals in high school. We beat up on a lot of boys in them days."

"Okay, okay, we'll just keep this little adventure to ourselves," Ketchum said.

I was surprised at how fast the raft was going, given that it was overloaded and sitting low. We were getting close to our takeout spot.

"Paddle toward shore," I said. "I see the truck up ahea—!"

"Aunt Nettie, why did we go past the truck?" Wanton said.

"Waaaa! We're going to drown!" said You Know Who.

"Crap on a cracker!" Ketchum said.

"He said a bad word!" Wiley said.

"When (gasp) does the Sisu (gasp) switch (gasp) direction?" Ketchum said as he continued to flail his paddle all over the place.

"Not sure," I said. "Maybe any minute."

"We're slowing down, Aunt Nettie!" Wanton said.

Sure enough, the Sisu stopped then the backwards current kicked in and started us back downriver, or upriver, depending.

"Well (gasp) it's (pant) about (wheeze) time," said Ketchum.

The Sisu River seemed hell-bent to get wherever it was headed in a hurry. There were a lot of ripples and we were tooling down at a good clip.

"Now watch for the landing where my truck is!" I said.

"We (puff, puff) got to get across to the (gasp) other side," Ketchum said, paddling for all he was worth. "Why isn't this (wheeze) paddle working?" He pulled it out of the water and all that was left was a stick. The paddle part was gone.

"Guess the duct tape didn't hold," I said.

"There's Aunt Nettie's truck!" Wanton said as we whizzed by the boat landing.

"Okay, okay!" said Ketchum. "Head for the sandbar (pant, pant) and we'll land there and I'll get *my* truck. Gimme the other paddle, kid!"

"There's the rock island again!" I said. "Go right! Get the poles and dig 'em into the sandbar."

Trouble was the sandbar was under a good foot of water and we lost one of the poles in it trying to stop. The raft floated right on past Ketchum's truck and as far as I could tell, was headed out to Lake Superior.

"She'll reverse again," I said. "We'll have another shot at it."

"Well (gasp, puff, wheeze), I hope so, 'cause Daredevil Rapids and Pinwheel Falls are around the next bend."

"Waaaaa!" shrieked Wiley. "I want Mommy."

"Shut up crybaby," Wanton said. "This is totally awesome, Aunt Nettie."

The Sisu was being a cranky ol' lady and didn't show any sign of reversing again before we hit Daredevil Rapids.

"Hang on to those boys!" shouted Ketchum. "Whitewater ahead!"

I grabbed both nephews as we began to rock and bounce through the rapids. Most of the branches, shoots, and leaves had blown off the Bramble Blind, and one of the crosspieces holding the boards together had come loose and disappeared into the chop. The tin roofing we'd nailed to the floor held good though, and we were still afloat when we shot out of the rapids.

"We gotta head to shore!" Ketchum said, trying to backpaddle, which just made the raft turn facing backwards.

Except I didn't see any shore to speak of. Just steep banks with trees leaning over ready to fall into the river.

"What's that noise?" Wanton said.

"Pinwheel Falls!" Ketchum shouted over the roar.

"Hang on boys," I said then picked up the one pole we had left. I could see the drop ahead where the Pinwheel Falls tumbled over a rock shelf. I knew after the fall, the river slipped over a rock slide that moved faster than the dickens. On each side of the top of the falls stood a few gnarly trees clinging to the rocky outcrops.

The raft raced toward the drop-off, turned sideways, got a little hung up on something, then slid forward heading for the edge. I lifted the pole and wedged it between the gnarly trees and she held. Me and the boys hung onto the pole and worked our way to the trees and grabbed on. The raft jammed between a couple of rocks at the top of the falls. But Ketchum got jerked loose, fell off, and went on over and down. He did a couple of cartwheels on the way down before he hit the white foam at the bottom.

"Wow! Aunt Nettie," Wanton said. "Did you see that?"

"There he is," said Wiley, pointing to Ketchum who zipped along the rock waterslide then splashing into an eddy where he swirled and bobbed around before he finally broke free and began to swim.

Even though CO Will Ketchum is a thorn in my side, he is kin and I was glad to see he'd come through the fall and was working his way toward shore. He dragged himself up the bank then got on his hands and knees.

"Ahoy there!" I shouted, waving. I think Ketchum waved back. Or maybe he was shaking his fist or doing something with his finger.

Then real sudden it got quiet. The Pinwheel slowed to a trickle, and the Bramble Blind broke free and was afloat.

"Climb on boys!" I shouted. "We're heading back to the truck."

"What about Officer Ketchum?" Wanton said.

"Oh, he'll be fine," I said. "There's a road runs not too far from the river, maybe just a mile or two. He can make his way there and hitch a ride.'

"Hey! We're moving!" said Wiley.

I was glad to see that Ketchum had dropped the paddle before he went down the falls. I grabbed it and helped the raft along. This time we were ready when the truck came into view and I had the raft on the right side of the river. It washed right up the ramp and bottomed out on the cement skid. I grabbed my shotgun and Magic Quacker and me and the boys climbed off and stood panting like a pack of coyotes after a long chase.

"Well," I said, "let's get 'er pulled up and back in the truck."

"Aunt Nettie!" Wanton said, pointing. "It's coming off the cement thing."

Sure enough, the Sisu River was done going backwards, or forwards—whatever—and the current had kicked in taking the Bramble Blind along for the ride. We all watched it move away, slowly turning this way and that, until it was out of sight.

Ketchum later said he saw what was left of it go over Pinwheel Falls, catching a bunch of air, and flying like a winged dinosaur.

## Banzai Bozo

So me and Ma were both thinking about spring. Ma was looking forward to planting a new crop of ruttabeggers. She always said that if folks could only grow one thing, it should be your ruttabegger. Truth be told, it was me who always planted the blasted garden while Ma supervised from a rocking chair on the cabin porch where she sipped iced tea laced with whisky. "Now Nettie, don't forgit to put 'em six inches apart. Won do no good if they's crowded." Blah, blah, blah. I just ignore her.

To me, spring means that the steelhead trout are running. The rivers were open and going like the dickens, so I was setting up my fishing rod and had dug out my hip boots, fishin' vest, creel, and lucky hat. Yous are never positive what the dang fish will be biting on. There's your plastic one-eyed lures, spinners, fish eggs, gummy worms, and contraptions with so many hooks and moving parts it's hard to tell what they're supposed to look like. And you can't trust so-called tips from others heading out to the river because folks'r cagey and sometimes give bad advice on purpose so's they can hog all the fish. I have my secret weapon for catching steelhead: Circus Peanuts and pork fat.

Most fishermen'r too lazy to bushwack. They rather be elbow to elbow at the Huron or Silver and pretend they're having some kind of special outdoor experience when they might as well be in line at Walmart waiting to check out.

Smartest way to fish is to avoid the hot spots and hoof it through a bramble patch or two then hike through a bog for good measure. I got a place that nobody knows about. I call it the Banzai Branch. It's really an offshoot of the Huron River, but I got the idea of calling it the Banzai when I watched two fools in kayaks go by. They were fighting hard not to go every which way and probably didn't know that just around the bend they'd find a stretch of whitewater strewn with boulders followed by a wicked slide and three or four small waterfalls. I figured that Banzai was a good name for the spot because anyone taking a kayak that stretch had a death wish, like those kamikaze Japanese pilots supposedly hollered during the war when they flew their planes into our ships. Well maybe wishing to die wasn't exactly the case, more like *willing* to die. Anyway, the pools around the bottom of the waterfalls had some good holes to catch trout. Of course steelhead were different. You gotta catch 'em making their way upriver to spawn.

Anyway, other than the two idiots in kayaks, I'd never seen another soul at my secret fishing spot, and that included CO Will Ketchum. While he'd be at the main branch of the Huron shaking down fishermen for their licenses and checking their catches, I'd be all alone to pull in some fine fish at the Banzai.

I was loading up my truck with my gear when the Alder clan came tearing up the driveway and skidded to a halt. My sister was driving and she jumped out and ran to the back door of the car and yanked it open.

"Hurry up boys, I gotta get Dad to the emergency room! Nettie, you need to watch the boys!"

"Dad cut his thumb off!" shouted Wanton.

"Daddy's gonna die! Waaaaaaa," belted Wiley.

"He didn't cut his thumb off—at least not completely," MarshMarigold said.

"I'm fine," bellowed Tag from inside the car. Hardly bleeding at—"

Then we heard a thump and when we looked inside the car, ol' Tag was passed out on the floor.

"Gotta go!" M&M shrieked and jumped into the driver's seat and peeled out.

I looked at my two nephews and said, "Why don't you boys go in the cabin and tell Granny you're gonna stay with her."

"Like hell!" Ma said. She had come to the door to see what the commotion was all about.

"Daddy cut his thumb off!" hollered Wiley.

"Not surprised," Ma said. "Dang fool."

We all headed into the cabin and the boys started rummaging around in the refrigerator.

"Can I have a beer?" Wanton said.

"No!" Ma said. "They's a Coke in there you can split and some of them dill pickle potato chips in the cupboard. Now tell Granny what in Billy blue blazes your pa did to cut his thumb off."

"He was helping me with my science project," said Wanton. "We were trying to punch holes in the top of a glass jar so's I could catch some mudminnows down at the slag pond."

"What's a mudminnow?" Ma said as she plunked herself down in her recliner and picked up the remote control to her giant screen TV. "Bring me my medicine outa the cupboard next to the sink."

"You mean your booze?" Wanton said. "Dad said you drink booze all the time."

"He does, eh?" Ma said. "Well at least I don't go and hack ma thumb off like an idjit."

"Anyway," Wanton said, "a mudminnow is a fish that lives in the muck and can sometimes breathe regular air, and can live in really crummy water, like a turtle. It hides in the mud then jumps out and catches prey."

"So, how did that make your dad cut his thumb?" I said as I chopped up some Circus Peanuts and chunks of side pork to use as bait. Ma always fried steelhead up crispy with some lard and cornmeal. I could almost taste it.

"Dad was jabbing the lid on the jar and the knife slipped, and he cut himself bad."

"Why was he jabbing at a jar?" I said, putting my bait in a plastic zip bag and tucking it in my fishin' vest.

"I told you! He was using the knife to poke holes so the fish could breathe," Wanton said.

"Figures," Ma muttered as she snatched her whisky bottle from Wanton and poured a goodly amount in her coffee cup.

"Well, yous all have a good time watching TV with Granny," I said. "I'm gonna catch some fresh fish for supper."

"But I need a mudminnow!" Wanton yelled.

"Well, I don't plan on fishin' at the slag pond," I said, "so guess you'll have to wait 'til your pa gets his thumb stitched back on."

"Well, they ain't staying here," Ma snipped. "Them boys talk through all my shows and if I happen to nod off, they's likely to get into mischief."

"My project's due tomorrow and I got the poster board all done. I just need a mudminnow!" Wanton yelled, jumping around the room.

"Can I have a Circus Peanut?" Wiley said.

"No!" I said. "They're for bait."

"I bet mudminnows love Circus Peanuts," Wanton said.

"Well, at least sumthin' likes 'em," Ma said. "They's disgusting."

I figured I had no choice but to take the boys with me unless I wanted to come home to a disaster.

"You brats can come," I said, "but we're going to my secret spot and if you don't catch any muckminnows—"

"*Mud*minnows," Wanton said.

"Yeah, whatever, anyway if you don't catch any, that's your tough luck," I said. "Now make yourselfs useful and get a couple of Cokes and grab those peanut butter and jelly sandwiches sitting on the table, and the potato chips and the Twinkies outa the cupboard. Go ahead and put them in your backpacks. How come your ma sent along your backpacks anyway?"

"We got clean underwear and stuff in case we had to spend the night," Wanton said.

"Well, take all that stuff out and put in what I told you," I said.

We crammed into my truck and headed out. "You two listen up," I said. "And quit smackin' each other or I swear to gosh I'll dump you on the side of the road."

"We're listening, Aunt Nettie," said Wanton.

"Now I got a plan so's we don't run into, er, any folks we don't wanna see," I said.

"You mean like the fish cop?" Wanton said.

"Yeah, him," I said as we pulled into the parking area at the Huron River.

"Wow!" Wanton said. "Look at all the cars and guys out in the river. Are they having a contest?"

"Sorta," I said. "Okay, so here's the plan. We leave the truck here, because Mr. Fish Cop knows my truck, and we bushwack to my secret spot. Ol' Ketchum will think I'm out there in that crowd somewhere and meanwhile, we'll be nowhere to be found."

"Cool!" Wanton said.

"Like hide and seek?" Wiley said.

"Kinda. Now get your backpacks and help me carry my gear. We'll sneak—er, cut through the woods here and find the game trail through the marsh."

Well, we weren't but a half mile into the woods when we hit a patch of brambles.

"Best way to get through these is to go backwards," I said. "That way you don't get your face all tore up. You boys lead the way and watch you don't sink down into some quicksand. I don't have a rope to pull you out."

About two feet into the brambles the boys start whining and carrying on. One lost his shoe and the other tore his coat. We got the shoe back and scraped the mud off. Wasn't long before we cleared the brambles and came to the swampy area. Best way to get through was for me to put on my waders and just slog through. Of course the boys didn't have waders and they got wet up to their knees. Twice I had to pull Wiley out because he was stuck. But once the two of 'em got muddy and wet—being boys with Bramble blood—they decided they were having fun.

"Way cool, Aunt Nettie!" Wanton said.

"I'm swamp thing!" Wiley yells, holding up his arms and growling.

We finally hit dry ground and made our way to the Banzai Branch. "Here we are, boys. Now you need to watch it. The Banzai is known to snatch young 'uns and take 'em down to be gobbled up by Nanabozo."

"Nanna who?" said Wanton.

"Nanabozo," I said. "He's a trickster that lives in the Banzai and is starved after a long winter and looking for some nice tender boys fer lunch."

"Waaaaaaa!" said Wiley. "I don't want to be eaten by a monster!"

"Then stick to the shallow water when you're looking for them musk minnows," I said.

"Mudminnows," Wanton corrected. "What's that noise?"

"Chainsaw, probably," I said. "Someone's cutting trees off somewhere I expect."

"It's getting louder!" Wanton said.

"That's just river noise playing tricks on the sound. See, now it's stopped, so hush, I'm gonna get my line ready," I said.

"Ready for what?"

"Fishin'," I said. "Now quit talking, Wanton."

"Wasn't me," Wanton said.

"It was a voice from the river!" screeched Wiley. "Bozo!"

"Been called a lot of names, but I've never been called Bozo before," said the voice from the river.

Uh oh. I knew that voice. "How th' heck…"

A small, goofy looking boat with "DNR Conservation Officer" stenciled on its side pulled into view and beached on a small sand bar at the edge of the Banzai.

"You like my new enforcement vessel? It's a jet ski. Works dandy on the river," Ketchum said as he climbed off and pulled the contraption up onto the sand bar. "It does a good job on a river or in shallows."

"But how—" I said.

"Hold on. I'm the one asking questions," Ketchum said. "I'll be needing to see your all-species fishing license that I'm *sure* you've got tucked away in that fishing vest."

I started feeling my pockets, pretending to look. "Well, I'll be darned. I bet I left it in the truck."

"But you said you didn't need—OW!" said Wiley as his older brother jabbed him in the ribs.

"Well, don't matter," I said. "See, I'm here helping Wanton with his science project. I mean we're *fishing* for marshmallows—"

Ketchum give a snort. "Marshmallows. For a science project?"

"I mean we're fishing with Circus Peanuts, for, er..."

"Circus Peanuts?"

"Yeah," said Wanton. "*mud*minnows, not marshmallows. I mean Circus Peanuts are kind of stale marshmallows colored pinky-orangey, but—"

"Mudminnows?" Ketchum said.

"Yeah, hee-hee," I said. "I never heard of 'em either." I gave Ketchum a wink. "But Wanton here needs to find some of these mushmellows for—"

"MUDMINNOWS," Wanton yelled. "See, I got a sieve to catch them and a jar to put them in."

"But we can't go in deep, because of the Bozo guy," Wiley said.

"Nanabozo," I said.

Ketchum had been looking from one to the other of us with his mouth hanging open. Then he kind of shook his head. "So you needed to come way out here for your, er, minnows and to find some boogeyman?"

"Sorta," I said. "Anyway, you probably have a lot of violators there back at the main run so me and the boys will just get working on catching the mud creatures."

"MINNOWS!" Wanton said. "They live in very low oxygen water and hunker down in the mud and wait for prey, like a turtle."

"That so?" said Ketchum.

"Yeah! And you can help!" Wiley said. "Watch for the Bozo guy and shoot him if he tries to snatch us and eat us!"

"I'm sure Officer Ketchum has better things to do than—" I said.

"Not at all," Ketchum said. "I'll just hang around here and make sure that the bogeyman doesn't snatch up any little boys. I figure it's my sworn duty." Ketchum said as he sat on a log looking smug.

"Great," I said. "Just great."

The two hooligans set out wading along the shallows running an old colander through the mud and sand. Mostly they found muck and seaweed and a few shiny stones.

"I found some gold, Aunt Nettie!" hollered Wiley, holding up a small pebble.

Most likely the kid had found some quartz. "Put it in your pocket to add to your collection," I said.

I went over to the dumb little boat and gave it a once over. It was kind of like a snowmobile, only for the water. I climbed on and looked around for the motor and whatnot. I was surprised that Ketchum hadn't tied her up. The Banzai did some weird things and the water seemed to be rising. "Hey Officer Ketchum, aren't ya worried this thing is gonna float—"

"I GOT SOMETHING! HELP ME GET IT—HOLY COW!" yelled Wanton. "I think it's bigger than a mudminnow!"

"Oh no!" shouted Wiley. "Maybe it's Bozo trying to pull you in."

Ketchum jumped off his log and ran over to help the boys. I heard him yelp something like, "It's got me, get it off, get it off," and so I climbed off the ski boat and ran over to see what was up.

Well, my nephew was right, critters do sit in the muck and wait to catch something, but it wasn't a mudminnow but a big ol' snapper that had ahold of Ketchum's thumb.

"You got a license to catch that?" I said with a snicker.

"Get this (bleeping) thing off me Bramble or I swear I'll throw you in jail," Ketchum said.

"For what?" I said.

"I'll think of something," he said.

"Hey!" Wiley said, pointing at the river. "I think Bozo is stealing your little boat."

We all turned to watch the ski boat drift off into the current and float down river. Well, Ketchum jumped right in, snapping turtle and all, and started swimming with one arm after his ski boat.

"Watch out for the rapids!" I yelled, as he swirled out of sight. I was pretty sure he could get himself onshore before the whitewater. Not so sure about the fate of the little ski boat.

"Hey! I got something!" shouted Wanton.

We all went over to see what he got.

"Tadpoles," I said. "You know, baby frogs. Look, they're starting to grow legs."

"Cool!" Wiley said.

"Good enough," Wanton said. "I'll switch my presentation. I need some new posterboard, though."

"And I got me a chance now to do some real fishin'," I said, pulling a Circus Peanut out of my vest and hooking it on my line. Just as I was getting ready to make my cast, we hear that buzzsaw noise.

"Hey! Look," said Wiley. "He made it. Maybe Bozo saved him!"

"More likely threw him back," I muttered as we all watched Ketchum tool past, full throttle, on his ski boat. He had one arm kind dangling down with that big snapper still attached. He gave me a dirty look and his face was all pinched and red. He yelled something when he went by and I don't think he was wishin' me good luck.

"Maybe Ketchum IS Bozo," I said. "I expect he'll be headed somewhere to have help getting that turtle off'n his hand. Heck, I coulda told him that you just light a match under the critter's chin and they let go right off but didn't have a chance. Too bad, because Granny makes good turtle soup."

No matter, though. I felt a tug on my line and a nice flash of silver broke the water just upriver. Fried fish beats turtle soup any day.

## Lucky Strike

"About three grand for the well, and if we do the septic at the same time, we can do it for another three thousand. Of course that doesn't include your bathroom fixtures and plumbing. That'd probably be another couple thousand or so, depending on how fancy yous want to get."

My head did some calculating and came up with a figure way more than me and Ma's cabin was even worth. Besides it was more'n our share. Way more. It would take us years to legally mine that much gold, even if we found some nice nuggets.

"I can write ya up an estimate. It'll be good for thirty days."

The fellow giving us the bad news about the cost of upgrading the cabin with running water and a septic system was Hempi Luppinen, a friend of my brother-in-law, Tag, the king of sewer sucking. Hempi put in wells along with septic systems that folks filled up and then Tag pumped 'em out every so often. They had a racket going, for sure.

"I might be able to give a ten percent discount, if it's a cash payment," Hempi added. I also barter. I'm looking for an ORV (off road vehicle) in good shape. Don't suppose you have one stashed somewhere?"

The only ORV I had was a fifteen-year-old truck with no muffler or review mirrors and an odometer that busted at 250 thousand miles.

"We'll give it a think!" said Ma, who was perfectly happy to have me tote water from the hand pump and move the outhouse to a new spot every year or so. "Ain't no rush. We's doin' fine with our path bath and hand pump."

"Easy for you to say, old

woman," I snapped. "You just sit around while I do all the work. Plus I don't appreciate having to dig a path through the snow to the outhouse all winter long. I got better things to do!"

"That so?" Ma said. "Like what?"

"Well, huntin' and fishin' and putting food on the table."

"Hah!" Ma said. "My gov'ment check puts grub on the table. If we tried livin' on what you bring in, we'd starve."

Hempi started working his way toward the door and muttered something about having another call to make. He left a piece of paper with our estimate on the table.

"What you want to waste that man's time for, anyhow?" Ma said.

My so-called highfalutin idea of getting indoor plumbing had all started when my two hooligan nephews came busting into the cabin a while back screaming about discovering gold.

"See, Aunt Nettie," Wiley had hollered. "I got two gold nuggets here that I got out of the Banzai River!"

What it amounted to was that Wiley took his rock collection to school for show and tell, and his teacher got real interested in a couple of the stones. Talk about a lucky kid! The stones turned out to be almost pure gold and worth a bundle. Also turns out people can keep gold they find in the Banzai because it runs through state land. There's some rules but turns out folks pan for gold—they call it placer gold, I guess, all the time. Instead of a few flakes of gold, Wiley got some dandy nuggets.

So I figured all we needed to do was go back to the Banzai a few times and dig us up some more gold nuggets and split up the loot. My plan was to use Ma's and my share to upgrade the cabin with indoor plumbing. I figured we could convert the gun storage closet into a decent toilet room.

"It's going in your trust college fund!" MarshMarigold had told her boys.

"But I want a jet ski, like Officer Ketchum has!" whined Wanton.

"Yeah!" says Tag. "That would be awesome."

Well the only solution that I could see was to keep the whole thing quiet and head on back to the Banzai to collect enough gold to upgrade the cabin. There was a couple of problems with my plan, namely my two blabbermouth nephews. First off, their ma says that we gotta split up the booty 50/50, since it was her kid that found the first couple of nuggets. Second off, them two boys are as likely to keep things quiet as to sprout wings and fly, so every greedy person in the county (which is most everyone) would be tramping around the Banzai, looking for gold. And third off, you can only collect so much gold each year off state land and can't harm the environment or set up a fancy mining operation. They leave that to the big companies, not us regular folks scratching out a living.

But I was good at thinking around things and came up with a plan.

First off, we needed to keep folks away. It wasn't an easy thing getting to the Banzai, but sneaky people would find a way by staking me out and following me through the bog. So I got to thinking about decoys. Duck hunters put fake mallards and Canada geese floating out in the lake so's the live fowl will think it's safe to land and settle in for the night. Then BLAM! You got a dead duck if you're a decent shot. Then you got things that lure critters into your sights, like bait piles, turkey callers, shiny fishing gadgets, and my favorite: Circus Peanuts wrapped in bacon fat. Fish can't resist it. So I had to mull over what I could use as bait to lure folks away from the Banzai River and the lode of gold nuggets just waiting to be found.

My second thing to think on was how to get around the measly amount of gold you're allowed to pull out of a river on state land. Rules say a half a troy ounce or 15.55 grams per year per person. When MarshMarigold looked it up on her phone, we figured half a troy ounce mighta bought us a toilet from the Home Depot along with a cheap vanity. That was a long way from digging a well and putting in a septic system, not to mention half going into some kind of trust fund for my nephews. The "per person" was where I was thinking the loophole might be. What I needed was a lot of persons that weren't interested in the gold, but just wanted to wade around in an ice-cold river and hand over some gold nuggets. Offhand, I couldn't think of anyone.

Of course the third problem was actually finding more gold nuggets. I didn't want to mess with measly flakes of gold that'd never amount to anything. Nuggets were the way to go, and they'd likely be buried in river mud and sand. Wiley had found his gold nuggets down in the mud when we were looking for some kind of minnow for his brother's science project.

Well, solving the first problem wasn't too hard. I told my nephews to blab to all their classmates that Wiley found the gold nuggets in the Sisu River, just above the pinwheel falls. Even during a drought, that part of the river goes along pretty good and folks would have a tough time getting there to boot. If they did get out in the river, they'd see a lot of glitter along the rocks that's a seam of quartz and fool's gold, or pyrite. It looks all sparkly, but it's going to be a chore getting it out of the rock and then it's not worth more'n a snootful of whiskey.

I had to give more thought to the second problem, which was getting a lot of folks to volunteer to mine for gold in the Banzai, keep it a secret, and turn all their gold over to me. If I could get a few volunteers, and counting my two nephews, me and Ma, MarshMarigold and Tag, we'd maybe have enough gold diggers to put modern plumbing in the cabin and send my two nephews to community college.

That's when I got an idea that I thought might just work. I'd round up some of the spunkier people from the old folks' home and give them a big line of bull. Maybe tell them that messing around in the mud of the Banzai would make 'em young again and take away their aches and pains. Maybe I could sell them the same bologna they hear on TV about drinking some concoction that looks like pond scum to shave years off their bodies. I wasn't sure how taking gold nuggets from them would work into the plan. I didn't want to cheat old people, so I'd need to figure out a way for them to *want* to turn the gold over to me.

So I met up with a gal at the Gnarly Woods old folks' home, Linda Figgy. We knew each other from when I helped out with a big party at the place. She didn't seem particularly pleased to see me again until I said I might take some folks—they call them Gnarlies—off her hands for a few hours. She warmed up to me after that and offered to lend me a bus to drive them. Turned out only three Gnarlies were up for the adventure, with the rest either wanting to play bingo or watch the afternoon movie in the community room where they had free popcorn and soda pop.

So we all loaded up in a sawed-off bus and headed out. Of course we could only drive to the parking area at the Huron River, then it was time to set out on foot. One of the Gnarlies had a cane and one had a gadget with four legs and a couple of bars across it to hang onto. Ma could of made it, but she was tipsy and decided to sleep in her chair. Wanton and Wiley were good to go, but their ma and pa bailed on me. Still, I figured I could put their names down for that half troy ounce each.

"Is the path handicap accessible?" asked the gal with the four-legged contraption.

I gave her a blank look, then the oldest nephew pipes up, "She means is it level and okay for a walker?"

"I guess so," I said. "We're all walking in."

We started the trek, with me and the boys leading the way and pushing brush and snapping limbs so's the old folks had an easier time.

"What in tarnation!" the man with a cane hollers. "This ain't no easy nature trail. This here is a frickin' bramble patch."

"Well," I said, "see we are trying to keep things hid from others, because there's only enough, er, magic mud in the Banzai for you three. We get us a big crowd, and there won't be enough gold—er, mud to go around."

"Tell me again about this magic mud," said another old gal, who I learned was named Myrtle.

"Yeah," said Wiley. "Tell us about the magic mud, Aunt Nettie."

"Well...hey folks, we're at the bog. So listen up. You need to stay on the trail or—"

"HELP!" hollered the man with the cane. "My foot's stuck HELP!"

"Oh shut yer yap, Bert," said Myrtle. "You got your cane on top of your dang foot. Now about the mud..."

"Um," I mumbled, "see it's only a story that's been going around, but there's magic in the mud at the Banzai. They say if ya mess around in it and look for stones, you'll be shed of all your aches and pains and feel raring to go like a youngster."

"Hey, kinda like them wonder pills they blab about on commercials. So, are the stones magic too?" Myrtle said.

"See, no, that's part of the deal," I said. "The stones kinda suck the magic out of the mud—especially shiny ones, so you need to pick them out and give them to me and the boys."

"Sounds like poppycock," said Bert, waving his cane at a cloud of mosquitoes hovering around him.

"I thought we were going shopping," said the old lady with the walker. "When do we get to Walmart?"

"VIOLET, TURN UP YOUR HEARING AID," said Myrtle. "HIKING, not shopping. Deaf ol' bat. The two words don't even sound alike."

So, we finally get to the place at the Banzai where Wiley had found his gold nuggets.

"Everyone should probably take off their shoes and socks," I said to the group.

"HOLES AND HOCKS?" shouted Violet.

"SHOES AND SOCKS," you dingbat, said Myrtle. "I got orthopedic shoes and compression socks. Someone's gonna have to help me get these suckers back on."

So we were all wading in the river, kind of running our toes through the sand and muck.

"I don't feel any younger," said Bert.

"Me neither," said Myrtle.

"I'M HUNGRY TOO," said Violet.

Wanton and Wiley pulled a bunch of cake and pie pans along with a spaghetti drainer out of their backpacks and commenced to sift through the mud. Wanton, the one who's got some hope at being a real boy with a lot of Bramble in him, said, "Got to get the gold—er, stones out of the mud before you folks can get younger."

So the old folks each take a pan and start messing around the mud. Me, I decided maybe it was a good time to throw a fishing line in the Banzai. I'd stuffed my rod and lucky bait (Circus Peanuts wrapped in pork fat) into one of the boy's packs and started rummaging around to get it out without tangling the line up more or setting the hook in my thumb.

"Hot damn!" said Myrtle. "I can feel the arthritis going out of my big toe. Hey, is this here one of them stones that kill the magic in the mud?"

She handed over a gray river stone, smooth and worthless. "Yup!" I said," and tossed it off into the woods.

"Hey, I think I found an oyster shell," said Bert. "I wonder if it has any pearls."

I set down my tangled-up rod and took the thing. "Looks like a plastic cigarette case to me," I said, sticking it in my pocket.

The treasure hunt went on for a while, but the old folks didn't find a single gold nugget, just regular rocks along with a snarl of old fishing line, a bunch of empties, and what looked like a piece off a boat propeller. I was doing some casting and reeling in and didn't so much as have a nibble, then my line grabbed onto something. It was either a monster fish or a blankety-blank snag. I worked the line real careful and felt a lot of pull on the other end. I was hoping it wasn't a snappin' turtle. Once it bobbed to the surface, I could see it wasn't a turtle and it looked like a box. Wanton waded in and grabbed the thing so I could land it without breaking my line.

"Wow!" said Wiley. "Maybe it's buried treasure."

"Naw," Wanton said. "Just some guy's ol' tackle box I bet fell overboard. Probably full of fishing junk."

We pulled it out of the mud and tried to open it, but the latch was stuck, or maybe locked.

"Well, if you don't all mind, I'll keep it and later on see if there's some tackle in here that's still good," I said.

"So when do we start gettin' younger?" said Bert, poking his cane at me.

"Well, I don't feel a thing in my feet," said Violet. "Does that mean they're getting younger from this magic mud?"

"My feet'r numb too," said Myrtle. "It's because the water's so blasted cold."

Just as I was thinking about how to get the Gnarlies back to their place, something rustled in the woods. We all turned to see what was coming.

"Bear!" Bert hollered, raising his cane and flailing it around, almost whacking Myrtle in the head.

"Hey, watch where you wave that thing!" Myrtle hollered.

"Well, well, well," said a voice. "What have we here?"

"Wow!" shouted Wiley. "It's the woods cop. Don't shoot!"

And just as he always does, my biggest pain in the patootie appeared from nowhere.

"Hey everyone," I said. "This is Office Will Ketchum, who has nothing better to do than harass a bunch of old folks on an outing."

Ketchum looked around all of us wading around in the Banzai and shook his head. "Bramble, what in hel—er, heck are you doing?"

"We got us here some magic mud, I guess," said Myrtle. "I think it's working because none of us can feel our legs anymore."

Ketchum's mouth hung open and he looked at us all like we all had a third eye in the middle of our forehead. "And may I ask what you all might be doing in this, ah, magic mud?"

"Magic mud, HAH!" said Bert.

"Well, hee hee," I said. "I'm taking these folks on one of those, um, viral outings and—"

"It's environment, Aunt Nettie, not viral," said Wanton.

"Right, enviral—whatever. We're just cooling down a bit in the river. We dug around and cleaned out some trash that I expect we'll haul on out."

"That so?" said Ketchum. "And you're doing this cleanup with a fishing rod?" He looked at my gear sitting on shore. The Circus Peanut was still attached but the pork fat was gone.

"Yup," I said. "It works pretty good at pulling trash out of the river. See the stuff we got?" I pointed to the small collection of junk piled on the bank.

Ketchum sighed and looked around again, shrugged and turned to leave. Then he stopped and turned back. "Hey, Bramble, any idea why there are about 50 people splashing around in the Sisu River by Pinwheel Falls? A couple of them said something about looking for gold. Of course I figured they were being wise ah—er wiseacres."

I shrugged. "Haven't got a clue," I said. "Gold? Ha ha! What a bunch of hooey. Wonder where they got that idea."

"Yeah," Ketchum said. "I wonder," he muttered as he vanished into the woods.

So going out was easier than coming in because the path was getting beaten down pretty good and the old folks seemed to be moving better. When I got them back to the Gnarly Woods place and they got off the bus, they stepped right out. Bert was carrying his cane and Violet had left her walker on the bus. Myrtle ran ahead and opened the door for everyone. Miss Figgy watched with her mouth hanging open. "What the...?" she said. "VIOLET, WHERE'S YOUR WALKER?"

"You don't have to shout, Miss Figgy," Violet said. "I'm not deaf. Hey! I'm not deaf and, for your information, I don't' need that contraption. I can walk just fine."

"Say, there, Myrtle," said Bert, "would you like to come to my place after dinner for a little nightcap and maybe watch a rerun of the Lawrence Welk Show?"

Myrtle eyed him up and down. "Maybe," she said, "so long as you keep your cane to yourself."

Then the two of them cackled like a couple of old witches. Miss Figgy just stared at them.

Me and the boys hopped in my truck and headed back to the cabin. When we got there, Ma was snoozing in front of the TV and MarshMarigold and Tag pulled up in their fancy SUV. We dumped all of the junk out of the boys' backpacks, including the old tacklebox that didn't seem to want to open. We squinted at it and saw that there was a lock.

"Need the key, or we'll have to break the lock," said Tag.

I shrugged and felt around for my Leatherman, then found the cigarette case in my pocket that had been fished out of the Banzai. I opened it wondering if maybe there was a good lighter inside but found a little key.

"Hey!" said Wanton. "A secret key. Maybe it opens a treasure chest."

"Sure," I said. "About as likely as getting enough gold to put in plumbing."

Ma snapped awake, blinked at us. "You get you any gold?" she said.

"Naw," Wiley said. "Just an ol' tackle box."

"And a key to a treasure chest," Wanton said.

Just for the heck of it, I tried the key in the tackle box, and it worked. The top flipped open and I expected some river water to come out, but it was dry as a bone and there were no lures or hooks or plastic worms. Nope, just a big old rock.

MarshMarigold peered inside. "Hey," she said. "I wonder if...no, what's the chance."

"Huh?" I said.

"Well, there was a theft a while back at the Mining Mineral Museum, and the thieves stole the Yopper Nugget."

"What's a Yooper Nugget?" Ma said.

"I read about it," M&M said. "The biggest gold nugget found in Upper Michigan. Like worth a fortune and weighs almost five pounds."

I picked up the rock and hefted it in my hand. Felt darn close to five pounds and it was knobby and bright gold. It was a nugget—a big one—for sure!

"It was on loan at the museum and the alarm didn't go off when they broke in. They think maybe an inside job. Authorities have been watching for the thieves to try selling it on the black market."

"Wow!" said Wanton. "Can we sell it on eBay?"

"Absolutely not!" said M&M. "Do you want your dad and me to go to jail?"

"I never heard nothin' about a heist," Ma said.

"That's because you and Nettie don't pay attention to what's going on," M&M said.

"You got any beer?" Tag said.

"In the fridge," Ma said. "Git me one."

"I read that there's a huge reward," MarshMarigold said. "The nugget was worth something like a hundred and sixty thousand and the insurance company is offering a reward of twenty thousand bucks, if I remember right."

"Whoa!" I said. "We could do the cabin upgrade!"

"Don't need no indoor crapper," Ma muttered then dozed off still holdin' her beer. Tag polished off his beer and crushed the can and left it on the counter then herded the boys out the door. "All this talk of nuggets has given us a hankering for some chicken nuggets from the Clucky Chicken Coop. You coming?" he yelled.

"Give me a minute!" MarshMarigold hollered back. Then she looks at me. "Fifty/fifty. We split the reward." She reached for the box. "I'll take it to the authorities and see if it's the real deal."

"Nope," I said. "I'll be keeping it here and you can have whoever needs to look at it come and take a gander and make sure they have the reward money with 'em, or I don't hand it over. And I'll put half in the boys' college fund."

M&M sighed and stomped out. Me, I went over and picked up the estimate from Hempi Luppinen and grinned. Ma could go ahead and traipse out to the smelly ol' outhouse all she wanted. Me? I could almost hear the new indoor toilet flushing.

## Bramble Lake

"I don't know why ya wanna waste good money for on an inside privy!" Ma said. "They's diggin' up the whole yard where I was gonna put a fruit orchard."

Ma had been talking about plantin' a fruit orchard ever since I can remember.

"And them trucks rutted up the path ta the outhouse," She snapped. "I'm like to fall and break my neck in the dark when I git the call a nature."

"Your trips to that stinky ol' shack are numbered, old woman," I said.

"Like hell!" You think I'm gonna use an inside crapper, yous best think again. And them damn trucks making more racket than a chainsaw convention."

Ma was simmerin' pretty good when MarshMarigold and Tag and their two rugrats came busting in.

"Hooray!" said M&M. "I *finally* won't have to be embarrassed—well, as embarrassed—about my family living like backwoods hicks."

"Humpf," Ma said.

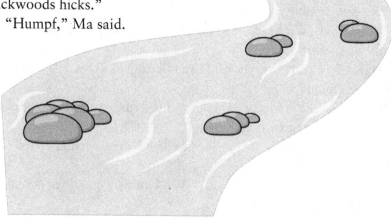

"Bite me," I said.

Tag and the nephews went over to the fridge and started rummaging around.

"Leave be the fried gizzards," Ma snapped. "I'm gonna heat 'em up for supper."

"What's a gizzard?" asked Wanton.

"Yeah," said Wiley. "Is it like a lizard?"

"Sure, I said. "You cross a grub and a lizard and you got a gizzard. Kind of smells funny but tastes like chicken."

The look on the boys' faces made Ma cackle.

"They go down good with ketchup," I added.

"So," Tag said, "when will you be up and running?"

"Humpf," Ma said, taking a sip from her liquored-up coffee.

"Couple of days," I said. "Something about a problem with rocks slowin' things up."

The truck noise stopped and Hempi Luppinen knocked and came in. He looked around at everyone like we had worms coming out of our ears. I guess we weren't what you'd call a "normal" looking family.

"Hey, er, how's everyone doin'?'" he said.

"Grandma's cooking grubs and lizards for supper!" shouted Wiley.

"Hush," said MarshMarigold.

"Anyway," Hempi said, "we got to put in the well before the septic, and there's a problem with the rig—well, not the rig, but the drill. I mean, the drill is hitting something solid, probably rock, and it won't go through. I demolished three drill bits."

"So, drill somewheres else," I said.

"Tried that. We keep hitting rock. Three different places now, about twenty feet down."

"Hah!" Ma said. "Maybe th' Lord is letting us know His 'pinion of this whole thing."

"Oh, pish posh," M&M said. "You need running water to be clean and cleanliness is next to godliness."

"Yeah," Wiley said. "Mom says we gotta take a bath or God will be mad."

"Well, if that's true," Tag said, "then I know a couple of Brambles that might be going to he—"

"Oh, shut yer trap," Ma said. "Them people in the Bible only washed their feet, and that was for special occasions, like lint."

"Lent, Mom," said my Perfect Sister. "And it was during the...oh, never mind."

"So, what's the plan?" I said.

"Well, I got a plan B," said Hempi. "I got a buddy, kind of a relative—goes by the name of Digger—who can see into the ground, or so he says, and can find water."

"Oh brother," M&M said. "Does he carry around a willow stick or something?"

"Nope," Hempi said. "Just closes his eyes and goes into a kind of trance, dances around, chants. Stuff like that. Truth be told, I've never used him because I always find water lickety-split."

"Well," Ma said, "your lickety done split. We ain't paying extra for no mumbo jumbo."

"No charge," Hempi said. "Digger owes me one."

"So bring him in," I said.

"This I gotta see," Tag said has he popped the tab on a beer he'd stole from the fridge. "And if you ever get this job done, I can take care of the plumbing side of things in the cabin."

"Oh Lordy!" Ma said. "First he almost burns down the cabin and now we're all gonna drown."

"Dad stopped the toilet from running at home!" Wanton said.

I happened to know that the only reason the Alder toilet stopped running was because my knucklehead bro-in-law broke some thingy on the waterline, which flooded the bathroom, and he had to shut the water off to the whole house until a real plumber could come and fix it right. So, I guess you could say he stopped the toilet from running in a roundabout way.

"Yeah," M&M snapped, "Tag's a real master plumber."

"More like a master flubber!" Ma said.

We all had a good laugh, except Tag.

Next day we heard a truck rumble into the tore-up yard and Hempi and this other fella got out and came to the door just as I swung it open. The Digger fella, I had to admit, was not hard to look at. The two came in and looked around.

"Mrs. Bramble, this is Digger Swiftwater," Lempi said. "He's a distant relative of some sort and works for the road commission."

"Hi folks," Digger said. "Hey, Tag, how's it goin'?"

"I *thought* the name was familiar," Tag said. "I run across Swiftwater sometimes when I'm pumping out the MDOT toilets."

"Yeah, yeah," Ma said. "Whoop-de-doo. I thought yous was some kind of a seer."

"Well, ma'am, I do some prospecting on the side," Digger said.

"Like for gold!" Wanton said. "We got a big gold nug—"

"Shush," MarshMarigold said.

"Actually, I prospect for water. The Lord gifted me with a sort of clairvoyance so's I can find water, even buried under rock."

Wiley looked up at Digger and said, "What's a claire—"

"Don't interrupt, Wiley," M&M said. "So, Mr., er, Swiftwater, are you licensed to—prospect?"

"No, Miss, I don't believe in getting a license for something God gave to me," Digger said.

"Exactly!" I said. "Same with huntin' and fishin'. The Lord put them there, and why does the state think they own them?" I was getting to like this Digger guy more and more.

"Now, if you'll excuse me," Digger said, "I'll just get started so Hempi here can get that well drilled for you and, er, get some plumbing in this place. By the way, I am a plumber of sorts too."

"Licensed?" Tag said. What a toadstool.

"Nope, side work," Digger said.

This was a fella I'd have a beer with, should the chance come up.

Digger and Hempi went on outside and me and MarshMarigold went to the window to watch.

"I think I'm having a hot flash," M&M said, fanning herself with her hand, which didn't do anything to cool her off. "Do you think he's Native American? I mean look at that long, dark hair. I'd *kill* for that hair. Ohmygod, he's built to last!"

"I guess he's okay," I said.

"What you girls doin' peepin' at them men?" Ma said. "Someone get me a bologna sandwich."

M&M left the window to fetch Ma her sandwich and I kept watching Digger and Hempi. Digger was walking around with his eyes closed. Never stumbled once. He stopped from time to time and dropped to his knees and bowed his head. He seemed be prayin' or maybe trying to get a vision. Then he jumped up, lifted his arms, then pointed to a spot in the ground. Hempi went over and looked at the spot and shrugged. Looked like there was a hole there where he'd tried to drill before he hit rock.

"You want ketchup on the bologna sandwich?" M&M shouted to Ma.

"Yup," Ma said. "And some sweet pickles and a slab ah onion."

"Make me one too, will ya?" Tag said.

Then the boys piped up they were hungry and pretty soon M&M was cranking out bologna sandwiches for everyone. Good thing we bought lunchmeat in bulk.

I went back to the window chewing on my sandwich and saw Digger go to the truck and pull something out. He went back to the hole while Hempi came to the cabin door, which I opened before he could knock.

"Okay," Hempi said. "There might be a loud pop because Digger is gonna put a little bit of explosive down the hole to get through the rock. He says there's a gosh darn river running below the rock. So yous might want to just let them little boys know it's no big—"

Before he could finish, there was more than a pop. More like a nuclear explosion that shook the windows and caused the dirty dishes stacked on the kitchen counter to crash onto the floor. Ma let out a yelp and pitched face-first out of her recliner but managed not to spill her special coffee.

"HOLY SH*&!" said Tag.

"WHAT TH' (bleep)," said Hempi.

"Oh no!" said Wiley. "God is mad because I didn't take a bath."

"Told you He'd know," said Wanton. "It's all your fault."

"Calm down, everyone," M&M said. "I'm sure Digger knows what he's—"

The cabin door opened and Digger stood in the doorway, and I swear smoke was coming off his clothes. His eyebrows were singed and he was covered with dirt from head to toe. His long hair had come out of its ponytail and was more tangled than my fishing line on opening day.

"Er, sorry folks," Digger said. "Hope that didn't disturb you. I might have had a little too much—"

"LOOK!" shouted Wanton pointing out the window. "A fountain."

We all rushed to the window and watched a geyser of water shoot 30 feet into the air.

"She should settle down after a bit," Digger said. "I think," he added. "I hope."

Well, it didn't settle down. The good thing was that the river that'd sprung from the ground was headed away from the cabin toward the gravel pit. I watched the outhouse wobble and float away, along with a few things that had been stored in the yard. It was a little troublesome to lose our outhouse before the indoor plumbing was set up. Maybe Tag could borrow us one of those plastic portable toilets.

"How do you folks feel about having a man-made pond?" Digger said.

"What about the (bleeping) well?" Tag said.

"Oh," Hempi said. "I can work with it now. Yous should have your four-inch well in by Friday. Or maybe Saturday. Monday at the latest."

"Holy smokes! The honey wagon's in the gravel pit. It'll be flooded!" my sister shrieked.

"(Bleep)!" Tag said and raced out the door.

"About this pond," I said.

"Yeah?" Digger said.

"You think it'll be deep enough to have fish year-round?"

"Oh, it'll be deep enough all right," Digger said, pulling his hair back into its ponytail and giving me a smile. He had nice, straight teeth. He had brushed a lot of the dirt off. "Nice pond attracts your wildlife, which makes huntin' a whole lot easier, you ask me. Hey, I have a fish hatchery out back my place. Nothin' official, of course, but I'd go ahead and stock your pond if you'd have a beer with me some time."

All in all, I was thinkin' the day had turned out pretty well. Indoor plumbing, eventually, along with the bonus of a private pond—or maybe a lake. I'd have game comin' right on the property. And maybe I'd have a beer with Swiftwater. I might have something in common with a guy who's got no use for licenses and could stock the pond to boot. I watched the gravel pit fill up. Yup, it was gonna be a lake, Bramble Lake.

# About the Author

*Roadkill Justice* is Terri Martin's third anthology of stories previously published in *UP Magazine* (Porcupine Press) where she finds an outlet for her humorous writing. She started her writing career as a regular contributor to several Midwest publications and has authored six books of fiction. Her stories often reflect the culture and characters she has encountered during her 23 years of living in Upper Michigan. Terri and her husband enjoy watching the menagerie of freeloading wildlife from their home on the Silver River. While the winters are harsh, the soul never tires of the beauty of the Northwoods.

Martin has a master's degree in English and has taught college success courses, tutored English at the college level, and served as an aide for college composition classes. Her middle-grade children's book *The Home Wind* was a 2022 U.P. Notable Book recipient.

Visit Terri's website at www.terrilynnmartin.com or e-mail her at gnarlywoodspub@gmail.com

Terri's books are available at Amazon or wherever online books are sold.

A suspicious death in a game processing meat locker is just the beginning of bizarre events happening in the Upper Michigan village of Moose Willow. It all starts when a mysterious woman appears at the Methodist church during choir practice. Janese Trout and her best friend, State Trooper Bertie Vaara, team up to connect the woman to a growing number of disturbing occurrences around town including the disappearance of Janese's eccentric lover, George LeFleur, and an undeniable increase in Bigfoot sightings. Meanwhile, Janese

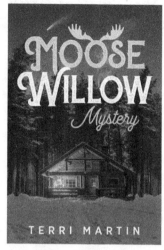

faces a multitude of personal challenges as she grapples with a sagging career at the Copper County Community College, an elusive pregnancy test, and a controlling mother who inserts herself into every hiding place of Janese's life.

"*Moose Willow Mystery*, by Terri Martin, lets cozy mystery fans know they are about to experience something wildly different with edgy characters, a big dose of humor, and an insider's look at America's best-kept secret the mysterious Upper Peninsula of Michigan."

—Carolyn Howard-Johnson, award-winning writer of fiction, poetry, and the HowToDoItFrugally Series of books for writers

"Terri Martin manages to present the ordinary, the bizarre (of which there is a steady stream), and even the violent in a way that will open a hilarious glimpse into the world of a small town. With brilliant characterization, she takes the reader on a wild ride of murder and mayhem, so let me warn you. Don't start reading until you have the time to keep going."

—Bob Rich, PhD, author of *Sleeper, Awake!*

ISBN 978-1-61599-689-6

Modern History Press

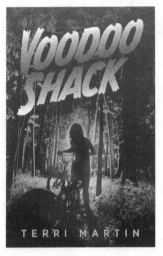

Join Iris and the Voodoo Shack gang as they investigate a mysterious death and an unsolved crime!

When 11-year-old Iris Weston discovers a ramshackle hunting cabin deep in Hazard Swamp, she and her friends decide it's perfect for a secret clubhouse. The gang dubs it the Voodoo Shack and meets there to swap stories and play card games. Ol' Man Hazard, the former owner, died under mysterious circumstances, and the kids speculate whether it was an accident, suicide or maybe even murder! The gang believes that cash from an unsolved crime may have been stashed within feet of the cabin. Even as things go badly awry, feisty Iris learns how to use her wit and independence to put things right, discovering what family really means in this adventurous and often humorous coming-of-age story set in rural Michigan in 1962.

"Set in the early 1960s, Martin's novel traces a girl's journey toward understanding the true meaning of love, family and friendship. Iris is an appealing character whose relationships with friends and family are realistically portrayed as she struggles to find her place."

*--School Library Journal*

"Martin has drawn on her childhood memories to create an engaging, feisty heroine, lively supporting characters and an easy-to-visualize early 1960s rural Michigan setting. And, although Iris doesn't solve all her mysteries, she finds the answers to the most important ones in this fast-paced story." *--ALA Booklist*

"Readers fond of lightweight mysteries solved by spunky heroines will take to this fiction debut, though a heavy ballast of tragedy and near-tragedy keeps it low to the ground. Some of the dialogue and set pieces show a promising authorial gift for comedy. (Fiction. 10-12)"

*--Kirkus Reviews*

ISBN 978-1-61599-720-6

Modern History Press

Jamie Kangas struggles with turbulent emotions caused by the death of his father, who perished in a logging accident--an accident for which Jamie blames himself. While his mother works as cook in a logging camp, Jamie is run ragged as chore boy. The grinding dreariness fades when Jamie meets a Native American boy, Gray Feather, who carries a burden of his own. The two boys become close friends as they face the challenges of a harsh environment and prejudiced world. And as trees fall to the  lumberjack's blade, Jamie hears the ghostly words of his father, warning of future catastrophe.

*The Home Wind* is a middle-grade children's novel (ages 9 and up), which takes place during the 1870s in a Michigan logging camp. Quality paperback, 198 pages plus discussion guide.

"*The Home Wind* is a beautiful novel for both middle grade readers and a wonderful a read for adults, too. Steeped in carefully researched historical events in Michigan's Upper Peninsula, *The Home Wind* is a delight. Martin's characters captured my heart and made the story come alive--two boys struggling to understand the world around them. This is also an important book for anyone interested in the history of Michigan's logging industry and in the Native peoples of Michigan. I highly recommend *The Home Wind*, and if you are looking for a gift for your middle reader, it's perfect!"

-- Sue Harrison, author of *The Midwife's Touch*

"Martin's descriptions of the scenes and action make a reader feel as if they are right there in the middle of it all. Readers can't miss the symbolism found throughout the book and a wonderful way to learn about the past at the same time. This book should go far, and not just with young audiences." -- Deborah K. Frontiera, *U.P. Book Review*

ISBN 978-1-735-2043-1-4

Modern History Press

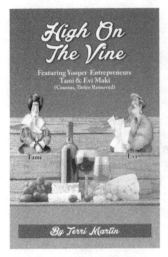

**High on the Vine features cousins Tami & Evi Maki,** who often contemplate the shortcomings of their respective spouses, Toivo and Eino. The story is told through a series of short stories set in Upper Michigan. The Maki women contemplate how their lives may have fared (certainly better) had they not married the two louts. After a hideous winter survival weekend sponsored by the Maki men, Tami & Evi take over the boys' hunting camp as punishment. After various less than successful entrepreneurial ventures, the gals finally hit paydirt when they form a business deal with a brotherhood of monks to open a winery, which produces a barely potable wine dubbed "Monk Juice."

~ ~ ~

My favorite episode from the book involves Tami and Evi dealing with the band of misogynistic monks who have a line of wines with names like "Resurrection Red Rosé", "White Infidel", "Pinot Gristly", and "He is Riesling". Terri Martin gets to show off her propensity for puns the best when Evi gets drunk at their weekly "teatime" which starts with boxed wine and ends with her passing out, most often. If you like a good chuckle about Yooper foibles and follies, I highly recommend *High on the Vine* by Terri Martin. Be sure to enjoy it with a bottle of your favorite beverage for best effect!

Victor R. Volkman, *Marquette Monthly*

ISBN 978-1735-2043-2-1

Gnarly Woods Publications

## A Disclaimer by Miss Bea Righteous

Well, my heavens! Where do I begin? First and foremost, while calamity may seem the result of my well-intentioned actions at the Gnarly Woods Senior Complex, I would like to make it clear that it is my mandate from above to protect the vulnerable, young and old, from taking that slippery slope into the devil's lair. Perhaps inadvertent collateral damage has occurred but I must preface the recounting of my struggles with the devil and his minions by declaring that I am held harmless from any and all such incidental damage or harm. Upon your wise purchase of this book (transformative!) and upon reading the chronicles within, I am fully confident that you will fully exonerate me from any wrongdoing and agree that I am on the path of righteousness. Though, of course, I do not expect any fanfare or meritorious recognition for my service

~ ~ ~

"Bea Righteous sees Satan just about anywhere and especially on those smartphones. There is no limit to how much damage Bea Righteous can invoke by way of her misguided do-gooder activities... a whirlwind of chaos surrounds our heroine... If this raises a chuckle, you are a definite candidate for the *Church Lady Chronicles*."

--Victor R. Volkman, *U.P. Book Review*

ISBN 978-1735-2043-0-7

Gnarly Woods Publications

Printed in the USA
CPSIA information can be obtained
at www.ICGtesting.com
LVHW091301271023
762201LV00006B/1206